The Cats that Walked the Haunted Beach

Karen Anne Golden

Copyright

This book or eBook is a work of fiction.

Michigan City, Gary, Lafayette and Rensselaer are real places in Indiana, but the towns of Seagull and Erie are not. The characters I created do not exist, nor have they ever lived in the above cities.

Names, characters, places and incidents are products of my imagination or are used fictitiously. Any resemblance to actual events, locales, persons or cats, living or dead, is entirely coincidental.

Edited by Vicki Braun

Book cover concept by Karen Anne Golden

Graphic design by Rob Williams

ISBN-13: 978-1723365263

ISBN-10: 1723365262

Table of Contents

Prologue

When Katherine caught up with Scout, the Siamese was very agitated. Katherine tried to snap the clasp of the leash on Scout's collar, but the cat darted away.

"Come back here," Katherine pleaded.

Scout ran and stopped in front of Cabin Six's side door, which was standing wide-open. She swiveled her brown-pointed ears forward then backward, in an inquisitive motion.

"Do not go in there," Katherine warned.

Scout rushed in and disappeared in the darkness.

"Just great," Katherine muttered.

Catching up, Colleen said, "This is creeping me out. I'm not going in there."

"Is anyone home?" Katherine called from the door. She rang the doorbell. "Hello, is anyone home?"

No one answered.

Colleen said, "Find a light switch."

Katherine found one inside the door and turned it on. She screamed and stepped back.

"What's wrong?"

"Look!" Katherine pointed at the man sprawled face-down in front of the fireplace.

Colleen gasped, "Is he dead?"

Katherine moved to find out, then heard something loud drop in the back of the cabin. She glanced down the hall. She saw the silhouette of a cat in front of a closed bedroom door.

"Scout, come here, darling. Come to mommy."

"Na-waugh," Scout cried. She stood up on her hind legs and tried to turn the door knob with her front paws.

"Hiss," the Siamese snarled.

Katherine dove for the cat, snatched her around the middle, and attached the leash to Scout's collar.

Scout shrieked.

Katherine thought she heard movement on the other side of the door. She held onto Scout and sprinted past Colleen. "Let's get out of here. Whoever murdered that man may still be in the cabin. They might come after us."

Chapter One

Mid-April

Return to the Pink Mansion

Katherine Cokenberger, thirty-year-old heiress to a fortune, finished surfing the Internet for vacation places in northern Indiana. She logged off, then joined her seven cats on the all-season sun porch.

She lingered by the door and reflected on how much the cats meant to her and her husband, Jake.

Scout and Abra were the oldest. The Siamese seal-point littermates once performed on stage in a magician's show. They had a strange ability to predict murder. Their death dance was a warning Katherine did not ignore.

Iris was a seal-point from an upscale New York City cattery, and one of the resident thieves. She served as a mother hen to orphaned brothers, seal-points Dewey and Crowie. Lilac, a beautiful lilac-point Siamese, was a gift from Katherine's former boyfriend.

Abby, a ruddy-ticked Abyssinian, was the reason that Katherine had given up her computer career in Manhattan and moved to Erie, Indiana, northwest of Indianapolis. Katherine's great-aunt left her a seventeen-room pink Victorian mansion, a huge inheritance, and Abby. The clauses of the will specified that Katherine had to live in the mansion for one year and take care of the cat in order to inherit millions of dollars.

Abby was the second resident thief, but her thefts were different from Iris's. Some of Abby's stolen objects helped solve several major crimes.

Katherine smiled, then stepped out onto the porch. "Hi, kids," she said softly. The cats ignored her.

Scout and Abra sat on the wide windowsill in front of the center window and studied the bird feeder below. In the corner, Iris, Dewey and Crowie occupied different levels on the cat tree, and were taking their morning nap. Abby and Lilac were perched on top of the window valance, snuggled together like a 1950s Lane Siamese cat lamp. With the attic office finished, the cats were happy to be back in the pink mansion, and so were Katherine and Jake.

Katherine's cell phone pinged. She moved to a wicker chair and sat down. She pulled her cell from her khakis' back pocket and opened the message.

Colleen texted, "Are you home? I need to talk to you." Colleen was Katherine's best friend since elementary school.

Katherine texted back, "Sure. I'm here all morning."

"Great, I'm leaving Daryl's now. I'll be there in a few minutes."

Katherine texted a smiley-face and slid the phone back in her pocket.

"Hey, cats. Anything of interest?" she asked.

Lilac belted a loud me-yowl. Abby chirped.

Scout and Abra exchanged a string of Siamese talk that only the two littermates understood. They jumped down, hiked up their tails, and trotted out of the room.

"Sorry I disturbed you," Katherine said, laughing.

Jake walked in. "Who are you talking to?" he asked, rubbing his eyes. His brown hair was sticking straight up from sleep.

Katherine giggled. "Medusa head alert. I hope you deal with that before you teach your class."

Jake was a history professor at the university.

"I think I'll leave it that way to see if any of my students notice," he joked.

"What time do you have to leave?" she asked.

"I figure I've got time to take a quick shower, then drive into the city. How about you? What are your plans today?"

"I'm expecting Colleen any minute. She just texted."

"She probably wants to talk to you about the wedding."

"You mean the part where she can't see eye-to-eye with Daryl about where it's going to be?"

"I certainly hope Colleen changes her mind about getting married in NYC," Jake began. "It would be difficult for the Cokenberger clan to fly out there—"

"How hard would it be?" Katherine interrupted.

"Hard on their wallets. Plane tickets and hotels don't come cheap in the Big Apple."

"But, Jake, it's Colleen's wedding. I think she should make the decision," Katherine said, slightly annoyed. "It's not just the Cokenberger clan, but Colleen has family from Ireland coming. Do you think they want to fly out to the heartland to see their niece marry in the place Daryl's mom and your mom suggested? Seriously, who gets married in a barn?" Katherine rolled her eyes.

"Wait a minute, Sweet Pea. Daryl and I checked out that barn. It's really nice—"

Katherine broke in, "Complete with chickens running amok, a couple of milk cows chewing their cud, and let's not leave out the slop hogs scarfing down the wedding cake. Colleen would hate it."

Jake laughed, "Katz, the place looks like a barn on the outside, but inside, aside from the shiplap walls and beamed ceiling, it's very modern with a well-stocked bar, a kitchen, a dance floor and enough tables to seat a hundred guests."

"Uh-huh!" Katherine answered slyly.

"Well, shucks pumpkin, the wait staff even wears shoes and everythin'. The tables even got them fancy tablecloths."

Katherine burst out laughing at Jake's fake country accent.

"Like I said, the place is really nice. And, the beauty of it is, it doesn't cost a fortune."

"Okay," Katherine said. "I see the two of us can't agree on the place for the wedding, let alone Daryl and Colleen."

Jake advised, "I'll keep my two cents to myself, if you do, too."

Katherine rose from her chair and pinched him on the arm. "What's the fun in that?"

The front doorbell clanged loudly. Iris woke up and growled. Dewey bellowed a loud *mao* in his baritone voice. Crowie kept sleeping, oblivious to the other cats' excitement. Abby and Lilac jumped off their perch and trotted out of the room.

"I'll get it," Jake said, sprinting to the front door.

"Send her back here," Katherine called.

In a few minutes, Colleen walked in. Her long red hair was tied up in a bun, perched on top of her head like a robin's nest.

Katherine bit her tongue from laughing. "Hi, Colleen. What's with the new do?"

"I wear it like this to annoy Daryl. He hates it when I put my hair up."

"Are you serious? Jake could care less about my hair."

"That's because it's so short. Maybe you should grow it out, so you could have a bun like mine," Colleen teased, patting the top of her head.

"Have a sit down," Katherine said, pointing to a wicker chair.

Colleen plopped down in the chair. "I'm fit to be tied," she said, squinting her eyes in an annoyed fashion. "That awful, obnoxious, over-bearing woman—"

"Who are you talking about?"

"Jake's mom, Cora. I could strangle her."

"What does she have to do with you?"

"Oh, she's conspiring with Daryl's mom, and the two of them, thick as thieves, are planning my wedding."

Katherine said facetiously, "Has Cora given you the big wedding book?"

"That blasted book weighs five hundred pounds and is so dated, the bridesmaid dresses look like something from *Gone with the Wind*."

"Yep, been there. Sounds like you have your hands full."

"And, the coup de grace," Colleen replied with frustration, "Daryl wants to have the wedding in a barn!"

Katherine smirked and didn't tell her friend that Jake and she had just been discussing the infamous barn. "May I make a suggestion?" she asked instead.

"Of course, Katz. You're my best friend. I trust your judgement."

"This has nothing to do with the wedding."

"That's a blessing."

"How about we do a girls' retreat with your mum?"

"With Mum? I thought you were still mad at her."

"Water under the bridge. I forgave her. It's been awhile since I've seen her, and I miss her. Wouldn't it be fun for the three of us to meet somewhere for a long weekend?"

"Where? I'm certainly not flying to Manhattan for a girls' retreat."

"I've done some research and found this bed & breakfast in northern Indiana. It's close to the Indiana Dunes State Park."

"The Dunes State Park? I've never heard of it."

"It's a state-owned park with several miles of beach on Lake Michigan. It has acres of natural landscape. From what I've found on the Internet, it also has spectacular views."

"Keep selling it. I'm warming up to your idea."

"There's a B&B I can rent for a long weekend. That's next Thursday, or is that too soon?"

12

"By long weekend, what do you mean?"

"We can drive up there Thursday and come back Sunday afternoon."

"How long does it take to get there?"

"A couple of hours."

"I'm just asking because I'm taking a speech class this semester. Next Thursday I have to stand up in front of the class and speak about modern day colloquialisms."

"How did you manage that boring topic?"

"We had to draw cards from a bowl, but I think the professor rigged it. I know it's a ridiculous topic, but I have to give a speech without using any common phrases."

"Like what?"

"Like 'shut the door'! My speech professor says I use it too much."

"Well, no offense, but you do say it a lot. Maybe you could come up with another phrase."

"I'll work on it. Anyway, back to your plan, I'll call Mum and run it by her." Colleen looked at her watch. "I better go. I'm done venting on Countess Dracula."

Katherine shushed Colleen, "Jake is still home."

"Oops," Colleen said with a big grin. "I've got a class at eleven, and I wanted to do a bit of shopping before then."

"I'll walk you to the door."

Colleen grabbed her bag and followed. Iris came out of nowhere and tripped her. Colleen stumbled, then caught herself before she fell. "Katz, your cat is trying to kill me. That was premediated."

"Miss Siam," Katherine scolded. "We do not do that."

Iris sassed a loud yowl, and ran to the kitchen.

"Sorry about that. I've learned to not get into Iris's way when she's headed to her food bowl."

"Shut the door!" Colleen exclaimed. "I mean, perish the thought!"

Katherine suggested, "Maybe you need to work some more on your speech assignment," then laughed.

*   *   *

Later in the afternoon, Katherine was busy in the kitchen preparing a tuna casserole for dinner. Before she started, she booted out the cats and closed the door so the felines wouldn't bother her. Outside the door, the cats reacted by howling like they were starving to death.

"Be quiet!" Katherine called through the door. "I'll give you a snack in a minute." It was never easy fixing a recipe with fish, because no matter where the cats were in the house, their magic noses would pick up the scent, and they'd be in the kitchen faster than speeding bullets.

Jake opened the door, and seven cats dashed in. They gathered around Katherine's legs, begging for a treat.

Katherine complained, "Gee, thanks, Jake. I had the door closed for a reason."

Jake smiled. "Maybe you should have a tuna alert sign on the door to warn me."

Katherine opened the oven door and placed the casserole on the middle rack. "How was your day?"

"Fine," Jake said, opening the refrigerator and pulling out a can of Mountain Dew. He flipped the tab and took a few sips. He drew up a chair and sat down.

Katherine dried her hands on a dish towel, then grabbed the cat treat package from a cabinet. "Who wants a treat?" she asked, walking the cats out of the room like the pied piper. Only Scout remained behind.

She gave each of the cats a treat and hurriedly ran back to the kitchen, shutting the door behind her.

"A lot has been going on today," she said.

"Like what?"

"This morning, I got a text from Mum. She said she's flying to Indiana, and—"

Jake cut her off. He shook his head. "She's not staying here."

"Whoa, let me finish," Katherine said, eyeing her husband curiously.

"She's not staying at the guest house either," he answered with great finality.

"I know that Mum has made some bad decisions in the past, but—"

Jake interrupted again. "Dumber-than-dumb decisions is a better description. For starters, how about when Mum was your guest, staying in your home," he emphasized, "and while you were out of the house, she disarmed the security system and let in a psycho woman who . . . shot me."

"Please, Jake, let's not go there." Katherine didn't like to think about that day when Jake was shot, and in self-defense, she'd shot and killed Patricia Marston.

"Or, the last time she brought murder to our home was when she gave that nut-job school chum of yours our address, which drew the Russian mob to our door."

"I want to put this behind us. Mum has been like a mother to me."

"Look, I know Mum is your best friend's mother, but the woman makes choices that put other people in harm's way. She's a murder magnet. She's dangerous, and if she wants to visit us, we can put her up in the Erie Hotel on our dime."

"Okay! Okay!" Katherine said, putting up her hands in mock self-defense. "I surrender, but if you'd let me finish, Colleen and I are meeting Mum for a girls' retreat."

"Count me out," Jake frowned.

"I said girls' retreat."

"When?"

"Next weekend."

"Where?"

"I've done some surfing and found a bed & breakfast close to the Dunes State Park. It's available for rental next week. I can book it from Thursday to Sunday afternoon."

"Na-waugh," Scout cried from the countertop.

Katherine glanced over at the errant cat and scolded, "Get down off of there."

Scout muttered a protest and jumped down. She trotted over to Jake's foot and collapsed on his shoe.

"That's next week," Jake noted. Looking down at Scout, Jake asked, "Do you think it's a bad idea, magic cat?"

Scout crossed her eyes, lifted her hind leg and began cleaning her toes.

"Okay, crazy cat, forget I asked." Jake grinned. "Tell me more about this B&B?"

"I'm booking the entire place, so it's just Mum, Colleen and me there."

"What about Scout and Abra? They'll freak out if you take off without them."

"The place has seven bedrooms, so I'm sure there will be plenty of room for the Siamese."

"So, you're taking all of the cats?" he quizzed.

"No, why do you ask that?"

"Because we have seven cats and you mentioned seven bedrooms — a bedroom per cat."

"No, silly, just Scout and Abra. I thought that on Saturday, Daryl and you could drive up. There'll be plenty of room."

"Sounds like fun. I'll call Elsa and see if she can mind the cats." Elsa was their go-to cat wrangler.

"I'm waiting on a text from Mum to see if she booked a flight."

"Where's she flying into?"

"There's an airport in Gary."

"Yeah, that's right. Been there once."

Katherine's cell phone pinged. "Speak of the devil, it's Mum."

"Devil all right," Jake said under his breath.

Katherine read the text, then sighed.

"What's wrong?"

"Mum's in a complete tizzy because she knows a better place."

"How would she know a better place? Has she ever been there?"

"No, but apparently one of her Irish friends has, and she recommended a vacation cabin practically right on the water."

"Nope, stick to your B&B."

Katherine read more of the text. "Wow, it has a screened-in porch. Scout and Abra will love that."

"It can be freezing up there this time of year."

"How would you know, Mr. Big Shot?"

"I've been there . . . in April, and it was colder than cold."

"As long as the cabin has heat and isn't sitting on an iceberg, I think we'll be okay."

Jake drummed his fingers on the glass-topped table. "The idea of you staying in a place that Mum recommends raises a big, fat red flag."

"Well, I'm in a bind. I sold Colleen on the idea of going on this little adventure. She'll be very disappointed if I don't give in to Mum. Colleen's all for peace and love right now so close to getting married."

"Close to getting married," Jake repeated mischievously. "They can't even agree on a date. How is that close?"

"You know what I mean!" Katherine retorted.

Jake was quiet for a moment, then said, "Do what you have to do, but take your Glock."

Katherine smiled. "I must be a very good salesperson. It took a while, but I sold you on the idea."

"Reluctantly," Jake said, getting up. "Is it okay if I use your computer? I'm lazy. I don't want to trek up to the attic."

"You spoiled rotten baby. It's fantastic up there. Margie did an incredible job."

Jake walked into the office, sat down, then called to Katherine, "Come in here, Sweet Pea."

Katherine joined him. "What?"

"Is this the place?"

Katherine looked over Jake's shoulder at the screen. "Do you think this is the vacation cabin Mum texted about?"

"The cats seem to think so."

Abra jumped up and tapped the mouse.

"Okay, it was you. Busted."

"Raw," Abra cried innocently.

Jake read the screen. "The cabin is located near the town of Seagull. I've never heard of it."

"Look at the sidebar. There's a map."

Jake clicked on it. "That is very close to the Dunes State Park."

"What exactly is a dune? I did a Google search and still don't know exactly what it is."

"Don't you have sand and beaches in Manhattan?"

"In Brooklyn, there's the Coney Island beach, but I've never heard of a sand dune."

"It's a hill of sand along a beach. They're formed by the driving winds off of Lake Michigan. I remember that some of them are quite high."

"Yes, professor. What is there to do at the park?"

"Biking, hiking, birdwatching, swimming—"

Katherine barged in, "Oh, no way, Colleen will hate this. She's not an outdoorsy kind of gal."

"Don't stick up your pretty little nose just yet. There are other towns and cities nearby. If you want to do the drive, Gary or Chicago are a hop, skip away. You'll find something to do."

"Doesn't matter. Mum is planning it, so I'll go with the flow."

Jake said, "Give me your hand, my lady." He grabbed Katherine's hand and kissed it.

She laughed. "That tickled. Why didn't you shave this morning?"

Jake ran his hand through his beard stubble. "You don't like my manly look?"

"Yeah, whatever." She headed to the kitchen.

"Let me know when you find out more about your trip." He forced a laugh, and tried to hide the fact that he'd be happy if Mum stayed in Manhattan where she belonged.

"Will do," Katherine said, stepping back to the kitchen. "Dinner will be ready in twenty minutes."

Chapter Two

A Week Later

Misty Komensky, co-owner of Seagull Cabins, sat behind a fifties-era metal desk in the office, and sorted through a stack of medical bills. Her husband Arlo was busy in Cabin Five. She'd join him in a few minutes to change the bed linens and tidy up the cabin. Arlo said the people who just checked out did a number on it. The new guests would be arriving soon, so the cabin had to be spotless. The last thing Misty wanted was a bad review on their website.

Misty fretted about Arlo's health. He'd been a healthy seventy-year-old until three months ago, when he suffered a heart attack. Now, thanks to modern-day medical technology, Arlo had the blockages cleared, and several stents later, he was good to go. Her only worry was he hadn't been vigilant in taking his medications.

Arlo's potassium level would fall to such a degree that he'd pass out, then the drama would begin. She'd call an ambulance, and he'd be whisked away to the hospital. In the ER, she'd sit by his side for hours, becoming angrier by the minute because if he'd only taken his pills like he was supposed to do, he'd be safe at home, sitting in his recliner, watching TV. Instead, every trip to the ER resulted in more and more bills. Even with Medicare footing most of the cost, the supplemental insurance had refused to pay some of the bills.

Although the cabins were paid off, there were taxes and maintenance costs. It was a struggle to keep afloat, especially in the winter when they didn't have the steady vacation rental income coming in.

To help reduce her anxiety, Misty learned of a pen pal program at a prison not far from where she lived. She began corresponding with an inmate named Josh Williams. When he was recently paroled, she'd asked him to come to the cabins and work for her and her husband. Arlo complained at first, but then realized he was no longer up to the task of maintaining the cabins, so Misty hired Josh to be the new maintenance man. Josh would be paid an hourly wage, plus receive room and board. He'd have one of the seven cabins to call his own. And Josh would have her whenever he desired, because ever since he'd gotten out of prison, they'd been having a steaming hot affair.

Misty didn't like cheating on her husband of five years, but Josh was just so handsome with his award-winning smile, his sense of humor, and his six-pack abs. She found that when they were together, she couldn't keep her hands off him. No matter how much she tried, she couldn't resist him.

She smiled at the thought of seeing Josh in a few days. It was convenient that he lived in Cabin Seven, which was the farthest cabin from the office. It was a perfect arrangement for their love nest.

She didn't smile long. Nagging worries just wouldn't let her be happy. She couldn't divorce Arlo because she'd lose money in the deal. She'd lose the income from Arlo's retirement and social security. At thirty-five, she didn't relish finding another job, and she lacked the skills and the education to find another manager's position. She didn't have enough money to buy out her half of the business. The cabins sat on a premium location facing Lake Michigan. In light of their private beach frontage, a realtor had recently appraised them for several million dollars. *Where would I come up with that kind of money?* she asked herself gloomily.

In the beginning of her marriage, she loved Arlo, but when he started smacking her around, she was repulsed by him. He was moody and quick to get mad at her for the most trivial reasons. He was controlling and wouldn't let her have friends. That's when she started writing letters to Josh, and in time, the letters got more and more romantic. Josh said he wanted to marry her. She'd said yes, but she'd have to find a way. Divorce was out of the question. Misty pounded the desk with her fist and muttered under-her-breath, "I wish Arlo would die."

Murder wasn't her cup of tea, at least in the grisly sense. She had to find a way to get rid of Arlo so no one would suspect her. She'd watched enough CSI TV shows to know that she'd have to be very careful. Poison was out of the question because if an autopsy were performed, the coroner would identify the toxic drug and she would be the number one suspect. Could she smother him with a pillow? She thought, *with my luck he'd wake up, realize what I was doing and beat the crap out of me.*

Misty wanted his death to be quick. Although he was a jerk, she didn't want him to suffer.

Last time she saw Josh, she'd talked to him about this. He said he knew someone who could get a drug that would cause Arlo's heart to stop, and the coroner would write *fatal cardiac arrest* on the death certificate. Josh didn't know if the drug came in pill form or had to be injected, but he assured her, either way, Arlo would die peacefully. She'd collect the life insurance, and no one would be the wiser. She agreed that it was a good plan, but wasn't sure if they should go through with it. She'd told him that dreaming about this kind of stuff is one thing, but actually doing it was another. There had to be another way where they both wouldn't end up behind bars.

The office's front door bell chimed and Arlo walked in.

Misty startled and snapped out of the reverie. "Hey, I'm sorry. I'll be there in a minute."

He grumbled. "Damn toilet is broken. Gotta drive to the hardware store to buy a new flapper. Where's that new guy, Josh? He should be doing this."

Misty paused and chose her words carefully. "He had a funeral to go to."

"So? When's he comin' back?"

"In a few days."

"You're kiddin' me? It doesn't take a few days to go to a funeral. Where is it?"

"Some town south of here."

"How's he getting there? He doesn't own a vehicle?" Arlo said, getting angry.

"I said he could take the truck."

"The new truck," Arlo complained. "Damn woman. Are you stupid? Why didn't you just loan him your Cherokee?"

"He said after the funeral, he was picking up his belongings from his cousin's, and my Cherokee wouldn't have enough room."

Arlo walked up to the desk, and glared down at Misty. "I'm not happy you loaned out our new truck to an ex-con. What was wrong with the old Ford?"

Misty frowned. "It's like a hundred years old. I got tired of it dying on me whenever I'd go to town."

"It's my vehicle," he said sarcastically. "You never drive it."

"Josh tried to jump it, but it wouldn't start. He thinks you need a new battery."

"Like he knows somethin' about old trucks."

"Ah-ha, you agree it's an old truck," she said lightly, trying to get Arlo in a better mood.

"Don't you get smart with me," he said, not in a better mood.

—

Misty shrugged. "The new truck is a tax write off. Is that enough to wipe the frown off your face?" she smiled.

Arlo scowled. "Give me a couple of twenties from the cash box."

"Why?"

"Because I can't find my wallet."

"Again?" Misty said, surprised, then laughed nervously.

Arlo was not amused.

"Oh, don't worry about it. I'll help you look for it." She reached in her bottom drawer and removed the petty cash box. She handed Arlo more money than he asked for. "Take sixty, sweetheart, in case you need it. And come closer and give me a kiss."

Arlo brushed off the invitation. "I'm busy. Throw me your keys, so I can get the toilet fixed."

"Sure," Misty answered. She got up, went to her bag, and pulled out the keys. "Do me a big favor? Fill my tank. I'm about out of gas."

Arlo grumbled something and left.

Her cell phone pinged. She looked down at the text, then her mouth dropped. It was Josh. "I miss you, baby," he wrote. She read it and thanked her lucky stars Arlo wasn't around to ask her who texted. She texted back, "Arlo just left. Watch what you say! He reads my texts sometimes."

Josh didn't answer.

Chapter Three

Dave Sanders, the new owner of Erie's Dew Drop Inn, sat on a barstool at the bar. His bartender, Eddie, was busy hand-drying glasses. A man in his thirties, with a shaved head and a chin beard, came in. He walked directly to the bar.

Dave turned to see who the newcomer was so early in the day.

The man sat down two stools from Dave and said to the bartender, "Bring me a Jack and Coke."

Eddie mixed the drink and slid the glass over to him.

Dave started the conversation, "Ain't never seen you in these parts."

"That's cause I'm not from around here," Josh laughed, and took a drink from his J & C. "I'm stayin' one night at the Erie Hotel. Just checked in. I asked the gal at the front desk if she knew where Stevie Sanders lived, and she told me to come here." Josh looked around the near empty bar and said, "Well that guy over there ain't him." He pointed at the heavyset man wearing bib overalls sitting at a nearby table. "Unless Stevie's gained a ton of weight, and gone bald, that definitely ain't him."

Dave didn't comment but continued staring at the newcomer.

Josh continued, "Several years ago, Stevie gave me an address at a trailer park down by the river. But when I drove there, all I found was a burned-out trailer sittin' on the lot. Hope nothing happened to him. Can you tell me where he moved?"

"Who's askin'?" Dave asked suspiciously.

"I'm a buddy."

"How do you know my brother?"

The man eyed Dave curiously. "Yeah, Stevie talked about you. Dave, right?"

Dave didn't answer the question. "When?"

"We were cellmates at prison. Michigan City? Does that ring a bell?"

"Yeah, so? What's your name?"

"Josh. Josh Williams."

"I don't recall Stevie ever mentioning you."

"He got out before me, and I told him when I got paroled, I'd come and visit."

Eddie piped in. "If you hang around long enough Stevie is sure to show up. He always comes in for a beer when he's done with his electric business."

Dave threw Eddie a mean look.

The bartender took the hint and stepped to the end of the bar.

"Hope you don't mind my askin', but are you fixin' to live in Erie?" Dave asked. "Find a job here?"

"Oh, no, I've hooked up with a woman who owns vacation cabins on Lake Michigan — up by the dunes. She's asked me to help manage it." He lied about the latter part.

"Just released and you're already hooked up with a woman. That's impressive timing," Dave noted, starting to lighten up.

"We wrote each other letters while I was in prison. She was my snail-mail, pen-pal," Josh began. "She's my age, but she's married to this old geezer who is just about ready to kick the bucket. She said I could live rent-free in one of her properties, if I'd—"

Dave cut him off. "Sounds like a good deal, but you need more than a place to sleep."

"Oh, she's paying me a handsome salary as well. It's just that I've got this big deal coming up, and I wondered if Stevie—"

Dave read his mind and put up his hand, "Stevie ain't in the drug business anymore. He's clean. You better find somebody else."

Josh became irritated. "I'd much rather ask Stevie."

"He'll tell ya the same."

Josh pulled out his wallet, and threw a ten on the bar. "Thanks for the info," he said. He slipped off the barstool and walked out of the bar. In the parking lot, two men stood by their trucks shooting the breeze. Josh moved over to them. "Howdy, y'all," he said in a fake southern accent. "I'm lookin' for Stevie Sanders. Know where I can find him?"

The man in the checkered flannel shirt and faded blue jeans said, "Lives next to that pink mansion on Lincoln Street. Got him a nice house."

"How far is Lincoln Street?"

The other man dressed in a similar fashion answered, "When you get to US 41, Lincoln Street is the first right after the ice cream place. Pink house is on the right."

"I thank ya kindly. Y'all take care now, ya hear?" Josh said.

He climbed into the new GMC Sierra and plugged in Lincoln Street on the in-dash GPS. He wasn't sure the yahoos he'd just talked to were telling the truth. He was wrong. GPS directed him to turn right after the ice cream place.

Back in the bar, Dave texted his brother to give him the heads up, but Stevie didn't text back.

"Dang, I swear Stevie never answers his text messages."

Eddie came over. "He's probably out in the sticks where there ain't no reception."

Dave's cell phone pinged. Stevie texted, "He's the last person I want to see."

Dave said to Eddie, "Okay, he got it," and then he complained in a stern voice, "Don't volunteer information about me or anybody else in my family. You got that?"

"That was stupid of me. Sorry about that, boss."

Dave finished his beer. "Another one for the road," he said, then he started laughing.

Eddie reached down and pulled a bottle of beer out of an ice chest, handed it to Dave, and then asked, "What's so funny?"

Dave smirked. "Stevie's done found him a girlfriend."

"You don't say," Eddie said, shocked.

"Yep, he's got a date with her Thursday night, except it ain't around here. He's got to meet her somewhere up north."

Eddie nodded. "That's good. To tell you the truth he's been pining for that married woman way too long."

"You mean Jake Cokenberger's wife, what's her name."

"Katherine, but I've heard Stevie call her Katz."

"I'm happy for my brother. He needs a gal to call his own, but you know who'll be the final judge of whether or not the new gal is Sanders's-worthy?"

"No, who?"

"Salina. She's very close to her dad."

"Yep, you're probably right."

Chapter Four

Katherine grabbed her keys and cross-over bag from the atrium Eastlake table, said good-bye to the cats, and walked out of the house to the carriage house. She unlocked the padlock and slid open the heavy sliding door. She lifted her Huffy cruiser bike off the bike rack, climbed on the seat and pedaled up Lincoln Street. It was a beautiful spring day, and she wanted a quick bike ride before she had to teach her computer class.

Heading back to the mansion, she saw Margie's Dodge Ram parked in front and Stevie Sanders' electric service van parked in the driveway. *Yay*, she thought. *I sure hope Margie is getting the rest of her tools.* Stevie had already removed his tools from the jobsite, but needed to deliver the antique-brass switch plates he'd ordered for the attic. Not seeing Margie, Katherine assumed she was already inside. Margie had a key, which she was to return this day.

Stevie stood next to his van rummaging in the tool box. When he saw Katherine riding down the hill, he called, "Hey, good lookin'."

Katherine was momentarily distracted and hit the raised edge of the driveway. The bike careened to the left. She flew over the handlebars and landed in the front ditch, which still contained last autumn's dead leaves. "Ouch," she moaned, rubbing her elbow, which was now bleeding.

Stevie ran over, appraised the situation, and kidded, "Dang, lady, I'm not climbing down there and messing up my clothes to help you."

"Gee, thanks, but shouldn't you ask if I'm okay?"

"I can tell you're okay," he said with a flirty look in his eye.

Katherine's face reddened. "Well, then, can you help me up?" She knew Stevie had feelings for her.

Stevie held out his hand, and pulled Katherine out. "Looks like you scraped your arm."

"It's nothing, but I think my bike-riding skills are in question."

Stevie righted the bike and rolled it to the driveway. He parked it close to the street, kicked the kickstand, then walked back to Katherine. "I wish I'd videoed that and put it up on YouTube. I'm tellin' you, that was the wreck of the century." He laughed loudly.

"Very funny."

Stevie changed the subject. "If it's any consolation, I'll be out of your hair today."

"Did the switch plates come?" she asked excitedly.

"Yep, is it okay if I go up to the attic and install them?"

"Thanks for offering, but that's something I can do. I know how to use a screwdriver."

Stevie smiled and handed her the plates.

"I better go inside and put a Band-Aid on this," she said, holding up her arm.

"I can take care of that for ya. Want me to kiss it and make it feel better?"

"Stevie?" Katherine said, shocked.

"That's what I do when Salina has a boo-boo. Ah, shucks, I'm just messin' with ya."

"I'll catch you later," she said, slightly irritated. She'd had several conversations with Stevie about his flirtatious comments and how they were inappropriate to say to a married woman, but she chalked up the latest infraction to Stevie being Stevie.

"Wait, I need to ask you something," Stevie said.

Katherine stopped and put her hand on her hip. "What?"

"I know this is short notice, but can Salina sleep over at your house tomorrow night? I've got to drive several hours to meet a friend, and I won't be back until really late. I just don't like to leave her alone, especially after what happened when Big Mama and Mike tried to kidnap her."

"Oh, darn," Katherine began. "Normally, I'd say yes, but I have plans Thursday. Colleen and I are meeting her mom for a girls' retreat. I won't be back until Sunday."

"Oh, okay," Stevie said, slightly embarrassed for asking.

"No, wait. I've got an idea. Salina and Margie's daughter are best friends. Maybe Salina can stay with Shelly. I'm sure Cokey and Margie wouldn't mind, that is, if they don't have plans."

"Ah, we ain't friends," he said in a quiet voice.

Katherine corrected. "We are not friends."

"Yep, in fact Cokey and Margie hate my guts."

Margie came out of the house and asked, "Hates whose guts?"

Stevie's face turned a shade of bright red. "Nothing, ma'am."

Katherine piped in. "Margie, Stevie will be out-of-town tomorrow night and needs someone to watch over Salina. He doesn't want to leave her alone."

Margie looked at Katherine, "That's understandable. Cokey and I aren't doing anything." Then she turned to Stevie, "How about Salina coming to our house for a sleepover? Shelly will be thrilled."

Stevie smiled. "I'm much obliged, ma'am."

Margie asked nosily, "Where ya going?"

"Up north a ways," Stevie said evasively.

"To meet someone?"

Stevie gave a look, started to say something, then said instead, "A friend."

Katherine rescued Stevie from the awkward barrage of questions, and took Margie by the arm. "Come in the back. I want to show you my garden. My iris plants are popping up."

"I'd love to see them, but I'm expecting a delivery at the new job site."

"Oh, okay, some other time then."

"This is my official last day," Margie said, extracting a key out of her pocket.

Katherine took the house key and praised, "The attic looks amazing. Jake absolutely loves it. The cats love it, too."

"Thanks, kiddo. My pleasure. Catch ya later," she said, heading to her pickup. She honked when she drove away.

Stevie wiped his forehead in an exaggerated manner. "Thanks for that. Margie missed her calling in life."

"What was that?"

"She should have been a detective."

Katherine winked. "No problem, but you owe me," she giggled. Forgetting her bike, she walked back to the mansion.

"Yes, ma'am," Stevie said. He returned to his van, then yelled, "I suggest next time you wear elbow pads."

"I'll take that under advisement." She climbed the steps to the front porch and stopped when she heard a loud truck pull in the driveway. The driver parked behind Stevie's van. She craned her neck to see who it was. Judging from Stevie's body language, she could tell he wasn't too pleased to see whoever it was.

The driver got out and walked over to Stevie. He asked if Stevie still had a connection at the prison's pharmacy. She wondered what he meant by that question. Stevie had been out of prison for several years. Immediately, Stevie started yelling at the man. Katherine didn't want to appear to be Margie's nosy twin, so she hurried up the steps and hid behind the front column. She continued to listen to the conversation.

"What the hell do you want to do with that drug? I want nothing to do with you," Stevie said angrily. "I've done my time; you've done your time. I'm clean. I have a daughter to bring up. End of conversation."

"Hey, man, I just want to talk to ya," Josh said, backing off. "It took me two hours to get here."

"Dave told me you were lookin' for me. You found me. Now leave," Stevie said in a tough voice.

"I didn't come here for a fight."

"Get out of Erie and don't come back."

Josh put up his hands. "That's a fine how-do-you-do." He jumped back into his truck, fired up the engine, and peeled out, running over Katherine's bike. He dragged the Huffy up Lincoln Street. Halfway up the hill, the mangled remains of Katherine's bicycle shot out from underneath the truck's undercarriage and skidded to a stop in the ditch where she'd fallen minutes earlier.

Katherine darted out from behind the column and ran to the ditch. Stevie was right behind her.

"Who was that maniac?" she asked.

"A bike killer," Stevie said, still angry at Josh.

"What?" Katherine asked with a shocked look on her face.

Stevie put his arm around her. "I'll buy ya a new one," he consoled.

"No, you won't," Katherine countered. "That idiot who ran over it is buying me a new one. I'm calling Chief London."

"Katz, don't call the law. I know this man. He's been in prison up north, and just got out on parole. This kind of thing could put him back behind bars."

"So?" Katherine asked defensively.

"Trust me. Don't mess with him. He's psycho."

Katherine brushed Stevie's arm away. "Tell me his name?" she demanded.

"He's just some nobody from my past. Let's leave it at that."

Katherine studied Stevie's face and saw how upset he was. She backed down. "I promise. Lips are sealed, but Stevie, I'll buy a new bike. It wasn't your fault."

"Thanks, Katz," he said shyly.

"Thanks for the switch plates. Give Salina a hug."

"She'll like that. She thinks the world of you."

"And, I think the world of her."

Chapter Five

Thursday

The Road Trip

Katherine and Jake waited on their front porch for Colleen to arrive. She'd called earlier and said her class had ended early and she was on her way. Inside the house, Scout and Abra stood on the parlor's windowsill and waited also. The Siamese knew they were going somewhere, too.

Colleen pulled up at one o'clock and parked in front of the mansion. She got out and lifted the hatch of her Honda CRV. She struggled with a heavy suitcase.

Jake hurried to help her. "You're only staying four days. Why are you bringing so much stuff?" he asked.

Colleen tossed her hair back defiantly. "That's for me to know, and for you *not* to find out," she said tartly.

Katherine covered her mouth to stop a giggle. "Hi, Colleen."

"Hey, Katz."

Jake wouldn't let it go. "I think I threw out my back lifting this thing."

Colleen punched him on the arm. "Okay, wise guy."

Heading inside the house, Katherine said, "I'll get the cats."

Jake loaded Colleen's bag in the back of the Outback, and walked back to the house to help Katherine wrangle the felines.

Colleen climbed in the passenger seat, and pulled her portable GPS out of her bag, then entered the address of the cabin Mum had texted earlier. She didn't want to use Katherine's in-dash GPS because it was easier to mute her hand-held one in the likely event the cats objected to the sound of the GPS lady.

Katherine came out the front door carrying two bags.

Jake carried the cat carrier, placed it on the back seat and bungeed it to the headrest.

"Did you get the litterbox?" he asked.

"Yes."

"Litter?" he asked.

"It's in this bag." Katherine handed him the larger one.

"This is heavy."

"I know. There's a five-pound bag of litter in there. Plus, their canned food."

"Hope there's room in the back with Colleen's giant trunk in the way," he said in a loud voice so Colleen would hear.

Colleen yelled over her shoulder, "I heard that. It's not a trunk, but an overnight bag."

Katherine chuckled, but didn't comment. "This is my official overnight bag," she said, handing it to Jake.

He moved to the rear passenger door, and set it on the seat next to the cat carrier.

Scout and Abra became agitated in their cage, and began to do figure eights in the small space. The carrier didn't budge because of the bungee cords.

Katherine said in a soft voice, "Girls, I want you to settle down. Mommy has to drive."

"Yes, Mommy has to drive," Colleen mocked. "Auntie Colleen is the navigator."

Jake held Katherine's door open, and she climbed in. "Do you have everything?" he asked.

"Yes, I think so."

"Didn't you make a list?"

"Of course."

"Did you bring your Glock?"

"Yes, dearest, it's in my bag, but I'm not planning on using it. Now give me a kiss, so I can take off."

Jake reached in and kissed Katherine. "You be careful now. Text me as soon as you get there."

"I will."

"Okay, Sweet Pea," then he said to Colleen, "Keep her out of trouble."

Colleen laughed, "That'll be the day."

Jake shut the door and waved to them as they pulled out. Katherine stepped on the gas and headed for US 41.

Colleen, still holding the GPS, said, "I know the cats hate the GPS lady, so let me know when you want me to turn it on."

"Sure, but we really don't need it. I studied a map. It's pretty easy to get there. We'll take 41 to Schererville, east through Merrillville and Valparaiso to 49—"

Colleen interrupted, "I hope you wrote that down somewhere."

"Nope, it's in my head."

"Daryl said something about an interstate route."

"Na-waugh," Scout disagreed.

Katherine giggled. "The Siamese don't like the interstate because of the loud trucks, remember?"

"How can I forget. Dead of winter. Snow storm. Scout started howling in Manhattan and never shut up until we crossed the Indiana state line."

"She did not," Katherine disagreed. "She howled until Ohio."

"Raw," Abra cried.

Colleen chuckled. "Abra, you weren't even on that trip."

"Wow, that was a long time ago," Katherine reflected, then asked, changing the subject, "How was your speech?"

"Shut the door!" Colleen kidded. "I probably got a C."

"How do you know?"

"I was so nervous. Halfway through the stupid speech, my note cards flipped out of my hand and scattered on the floor in front of me. This obnoxious guy in the back started laughing. It really tripped me up."

"Did you finish it?"

"I did, after a few agonizing minutes. I'm so glad I'd memorized it."

"So why would you get a C?"

"C for clutz."

"I think that word is spelled with a K."

"Oh, okay. Can you get a K on something?"

Colleen tipped her head back and laughed.

*   *   *

Two-and-a-half hours into the trip, with heavy

traffic on US 30, Katherine spotted a service station. The

place was bustling with people pumping gas or going inside

to the convenience store. She drove in and parked at the

only available pump.

Colleen had dozed off and woke up with a start.

"Are we there?"

"No, we still have several miles to go."

"I must have fallen asleep."

"Lucky you. Scout and Abra didn't quiet down

until Valparaiso."

"Wherever that is," Colleen said, getting out. "I'm

going to use the bat room."

Katherine laughed at her friend's pronunciation.

"You mean bathroom?"

"That's what I said," Colleen answered, leaving.

Katherine got out, too, removed the gas nozzle from

the pump, and began filling the Subaru. She looked

through the back window to check on the cats.

53

Scout and Abra were exhausted from screeching at every vehicle that passed by. They were now spooned together, and woke up when they heard Katherine's voice.

"Waugh," Scout cried sleepily, which sounded like "are we there yet?"

Katherine called through the window. 'We should be there in less than thirty minutes. Will that make my darlings happy?"

"Raw," Abra answered, blinking an eye kiss.

Colleen returned to the vehicle holding several tourist fliers in her hand. "Katz, there's a ghost tour on the beach. We have to check it out," she said excitedly.

"Cool," Katherine said, climbing back into the Outback. Colleen did the same.

Katherine started the engine and drove back onto US 30. "Start looking for signs to State Road 49."

"Shouldn't I turn on the GPS?"

"Not until we get to Seagull. The cats just quieted down. I need to give my ears a rest."

"Okay, but the sign back there said 49 was in ten miles."

"Really? I didn't see a sign."

"The sign was big as a bus."

Katherine sighed. "I'm getting hungry."

"Me, too."

"We just passed every conceivable fast food restaurant known to man, but I didn't want to wake you."

"Maybe there's a burger place in Seagull—"

"With a drive-through," Katherine added. "So, we don't have to go inside. We can take food to the cabin. Take Mum something."

"Sure."

"Have you heard from Mum? I don't know why I didn't ask earlier."

"I got a text before we left Erie. Her flight landed in Gary and she was taking a limo service to the cabin."

"A limo? Won't that be expensive?"

Colleen shrugged. "I don't argue with Mum."

"Looks like she could have taken a bus or train or something," Katherine digressed. "Did she text you to say she'd arrived at the cabin?"

"No, but I assume she did," Colleen said. "Let me read this about the ghost tour," she said, picking up the flier. "Wow, did you know that where we're going has a very famous ghost legend?"

"The Dunes State Park?"

Colleen nodded and said in a spooky voice, "The spirit roams the beach by the Dunes State Park."

"That's close to Seagull."

Colleen read out loud, "In 1915, a woman used to swim nude in Lake Michigan by the Dunes State Park. Fishermen began spreading news about it, and curiosity-seekers flocked to the area to try and spot Diana."

"Voyeurs," Katherine noted.

"Her real name was Alice Gray."

"If her name was Alice, why do people call her Diana?"

"The fishermen named her. They said she was like the ancient goddess Diana."

"So, when did Diana become a ghost, I mean, spirit?"

Colleen read in silence, then said, "She was highly educated, came from a wealthy family in Chicago, and decided she wanted a private life on the Indiana dunes rather than the hustle and bustle of the city. She died in 1925 of kidney failure."

"How does dying from natural causes make her a spirit?" Katherine asked skeptically. "Did she drown? Was she murdered? Did something traumatic happen that caused her to haunt the living?"

Colleen didn't answer and kept reading. "Oh, this is sad," she continued. "Before she died in her husband's arms, she wished to be cremated and her ashes thrown along the sand dunes she loved. Instead, she was buried in a cemetery in Gary, Indiana."

"So, Alice didn't like the way her burial wishes were carried out? Makes no sense."

"Actually, it does make sense. Alice is tied to the location of her death, which was in her hut on the beach."

"Okay, we can do the ghost tour."

"Darn, they only do tours in the summer."

Katherine said, looking for road signs, "Did we pass our exit? I've been so into your Diana story, I haven't been paying attention to the signs."

Colleen looked out her window and said eagerly, "There it is. Exit in a half mile."

"Which lane though?" Katherine asked.

"Can I turn on the GPS lady now?"

"Yes."

Colleen turned the device on, and the GPS lady droned, "Turn left at State Road 49."

"Oh, darn. I'm in the wrong lane."

"Get over! Get over!"

"Too late. I'll turn around and go back."

Scout and Abra began shrieking in their cat carrier.

"Calm down, my treasures," Katherine cooed. She turned around in a restaurant parking lot and headed back.

"Recalculating," the GPS lady droned.

Katherine took the exit and merged into traffic.

"Okay, we're on 49, now what?" Colleen asked.

Katherine didn't answer. "I . . . forget."

"I thought you wrote it down."

"I never said that."

"No problem. I plugged in the address before we left Erie." Colleen checked the GPS screen. "We're about eight miles from Seagull, and thirteen miles from the cabins."

"What was the address again?"

"1313 Beaches Lane. That address cracks me up," Colleen said. "It reminds me of that old TV show — *The Munsters*."

"But, wasn't their address 1313 Mockingbird Lane?"

"1313," Colleen giggled.

Katherine drove several more miles, then worried, "I wonder if the GPS is wrong. The website said the cabins were right outside of Seagull. We're coming up on Seagull now. Five more miles to the cabins doesn't make any sense."

"Let's just do what the GPS lady wants."

Katherine drove through the town. She spotted a McDonald's on the right. She slowed down, then drove past it.

Colleen asked, "What are you doing? I thought we were picking up food."

"I changed my mind. I'd much rather get the cats situated and then come back. Is that okay?"

"I suppose, but I'm starving to death. I haven't eaten since breakfast."

Katherine drove out of the town limits. "I thought Erie was small. This town wins the prize."

The Siamese din had reached an ear-splitting crescendo.

Colleen put her hands over her ears.

"Girls, be quiet," Katherine said, annoyed.

"Turn right at Beaches Lane," the GPS lady said.

Katherine tapped the brakes and slowed down. She turned into a single lane, sand-covered road that had a number of small branches strewn across it.

Colleen looked out her window, "This road doesn't look like it's been travelled since the dinosaurs roamed the planet."

Katherine swerved to avoid hitting a large pothole.

Scout and Abra hissed.

"Katz, tell me again why we brought them?" Colleen complained.

"They'll settle down once we get to the cabin."

"I don't see any signs of life here."

"Did you enter the right address?"

"Yes," Colleen said defensively. "Mum texted it to me."

Katherine rounded a bend and jammed on the brakes. A large tree had fallen and blocked the road.

The cats stopped shrieking and became very quiet.

Looming twenty yards from the road was a two-story, mansard-roofed Victorian house. The house was in various stages of decrepitude. Windows were broken out and some of them were boarded-up. The place hadn't seen a coat of paint since the 1890s. A rusted pickup truck graced the overgrown yard.

"Oh, my," Katherine said. "What a dump!"

"I can't breathe," Colleen said, laughing. She fanned her face. "Mum is so daft. She gave us the wrong address."

"I'd say. Chalk one up for Mum. Now help me navigate back to where we came from."

"Ma-waugh," Scout agreed.

Colleen noted, "There's no place to turn around."

"I know. I'll have to back up." Katherine put the Outback in reverse and cautiously backed down the lane. She stopped before she backed onto the highway. "Look your way. Any one coming?"

"No, go for it."

She carefully entered the highway, then headed back to Seagull. She glanced over at Colleen, who was busy punching in a message on her cell phone.

Colleen sent the text, then in a few seconds she got an answer. She laughed. "Mum says the address is 1315 Beach Road."

"Okay, I know where it is. I saw the sign just outside of town."

In a few minutes, Katherine was driving down a paved, heavily wooded, tree-lined road. "I wonder why it's named Beach Road, when all I see are trees."

"Over there," Colleen said, pointing. "That looks like a sand dune."

"With trees on it? I guess I expected a dune to look like something from the Sahara Desert."

"Yeah, and I thought the road would front the lake."

Katherine slowed the SUV down. "I see a sliver of blue. That must be the lake."

Colleen admired, "I could live here."

"Not sure what the winter is like," Katherine said.

A few miles further they spotted a sign to the cabins.

Colleen laughed, "Seagull Cabins. Too funny. Everything around here is named Seagull."

The cabins were tucked between two high dunes, and barely could be seen from the road.

Katherine slowed down to a crawl.

"There's a lane. Turn. Turn."

Katherine drove onto a lane that was partially covered with sand. When she reached the rise, she could see a service road that ran behind the cabins.

"Which one is it?" Colleen asked.

"The first one is the manager's, the second one has a car parked in back of it. Mum used a limo service. That can't be it," Katherine thought out loud. "Hey, there's Mum."

Mum was sitting outside the third cabin, on a folding lawn chair. She was drinking from a tall, fifties-style aluminum tumbler.

Katherine pulled in and parked.

"I can't see the lake," Colleen complained.

"You probably can from the front of the cabin."

Colleen jumped out of the SUV and ran to her mother.

"Aw, sweet girl. I've missed you," Mum said.

Mum hugged Colleen, then turned to Katherine, who had just gotten out of the car, "Katz, get over here. Group hug," she said happily in her Irish brogue. "I'm so glad to see me girls again."

"Mum, how was your flight?" Colleen asked.

"The turbulence was dreadful. I thought I'd died in me bed."

Katherine laughed. "I'm going to run in and check out the room the cats will be in." She darted into the cabin.

Mum said sheepishly to Colleen. "There's a bit of a problem. I thought the cabin had three bedrooms."

"And?" Colleen asked tartly.

"There's only two. You're going to have to share a—"

Colleen interrupted, "Room with Katz and her cats. Oh, no, no."

"Just go inside and look," Mum said. "Off you go."

Katherine glanced into the first bedroom. Mum's suitcase was on the bed, along with several plastic bags from a store in Gary called Bigmart.

"That's not it," she said, moving to the second bedroom. Entering the room, she was taken aback by how small it was. "Geez, this is like a walk-in closet."

A rustic-looking bunk bed was positioned against the wall. There was a three-drawer dresser and mirror. The window was the kind that cranked open, but didn't have a handle. A pair of pliers rested on the windowsill. Katherine assumed that was how one turned the crank.

Colleen walked in. "Oh, this is awful."

"Shhh, Mum will hear you," Katherine said. "We don't want to hurt her feelings."

"Well, it *is* awful. Besides, she's outside watching the cats until we come back."

"Good plan," Katherine said, then added, "I've never slept on a bunk bed."

"I get the top."

Katherine thought, *why does she want to sleep in here when she has her own room,* but asked instead, "And, why do you get the top, carrot top?"

"Because I've never slept on the top of a bunk bed before."

"Like you've slept on a bunk bed before."

"But I have," Colleen insisted. "I have brothers. When we were young, Mum lived in a two-bedroom apartment. In one of the bedrooms there were two bunk beds. That's where my brothers slept. I shared the second bedroom with Mum. The room was too small to fit two beds, so Mum bought another bunk bed. She slept on the top bunk and I slept on the bottom one."

"How do you remember that far back? I can't remember anything."

"I'm a genius."

Katherine cracked up. "Okay, you can have the top and I'll have the bottom. I'm not sure why you want to sleep in my room when you have your own."

"That's the bad news."

"What?"

"There isn't a third bedroom."

"No, way!"

"Mum just told me."

"Okay, then the cats will have to stay in here with us."

"In here with us," Colleen disapproved. "Why don't you put them in the bathroom?"

"And, have them shriek all night? Not a good idea. Look, you'll be on the top bunk. They won't bother you up there."

"How do you know? They're like little monkeys. They'll be climbing all over me when I'm trying to sleep."

"I won't let them do that, besides they'll be sleeping with me. Here quick. Help me cat-proof." Katherine got down on her hands and knees and peered under the bed. She saw a small, white object and picked it up. "This won't do. It's a Tylenol."

"Isn't that poisonous to cats?"

"Yep. Let me see if there are any more where that came from. Let's comb the rug."

After several minutes, and a short sneezing fit by Colleen, the two decided the room was fit for the cats. They walked outside to bring them in.

Chapter Six

Katherine and Colleen each poured into an Adirondack chair on the cabin's screened-in porch. The Siamese were instantly drawn to the warm, cozy blankets that mum brought to the girls. Katherine held Scout on her lap; Colleen held Abra. The porch heater was on full-force, and with the overhead ceiling fan blowing the warm air down, the porch was tolerable.

Colleen said, "Abra, can you move a bit? My legs are asleep."

"Raw," the Siamese protested.

"Darling, lass, I just want to check my phone."

"Are you expecting a text from Deputy Dreamboat?" Katherine asked nosily.

"No, not this time. I told Daryl not to text me here unless it was an emergency. Besides he's working the night shift, so I never bother him."

"When did he start working the night shift?"

"He's covering for another deputy whose wife just had a baby."

"Cool."

"I'm checking the weather app. I want to find out the temperature."

"I can tell you that info. It's nippy."

Colleen looked up from her cell phone. "It's forty degrees."

"But I'm banking the wind chill off the lake makes it feel colder."

Mum walked onto the porch carrying a boxed wine. She set it down on a crudely-made side table.

"What's that?" Colleen asked.

Mum answered, "Oh, it's just one of those box wines. You know, the cheap kind. It doesn't have as much alcohol as the bottled kind."

Katherine moved her feet off the ottoman and wondered when the argument would begin. Mum had been off alcohol for several years.

Colleen's face turned red. "Mum, what are you thinking? That boxed wine has just as much alcohol as bottled wine."

Mum laughed. "So, me daughter is a wine expert now." Mum engaged the tap and poured two glasses. "Here, Katz," she said, handing Katherine a glass.

"Thanks, Mum," Katherine said, then looked at Colleen to see when her friend would blow up.

Colleen did a side glance to Katherine. She shook her head. "I don't think I want any," she said.

Mum poured her a goblet anyway. "It's a retreat. Let's be merry and not so gloomy. You're finally getting married to that lad who looks like he stepped off the red carpet."

Katherine smiled. "What's that mean?"

"Oh, before the Academy Awards ceremony, the movie stars walk on a red carpet. All the men are so handsome. Here take it," Mum said placing the goblet in Colleen's hand.

Colleen took a sip, "Eh gads, Mum. This is so sweet."

"I know. The sugar helps counteract the effects of the alcohol."

Katherine mouthed the words to Colleen, *That's ridiculous.*

Mum found a nearby chair and sat down. She carried an aluminum tumbler in her hand.

Colleen asked Mum, suspiciously, "What are you drinking?"

"A bit of apple juice," Mum defended. "I'd offer you some, but I drank the entire jug today."

"Wine? Apple juice? How did you get that stuff? You don't have a car?"

"Oh, I paid the limo service driver extra if I could run into a market and buy a few things."

Katherine said, "That was thoughtful. Thanks, Mum."

"He drove into this parking lot in front of this huge store. I swear it took me an hour just to walk through it."

"I saw the Bigmart bags on your bed," Katherine said.

"I bought the basics: bread, milk, tea, and eggs. Plus, a few other sundries."

Colleen, relieved that Mum was drinking apple juice, said, "I love the sound the waves make on the beach."

Katherine answered, "I could listen to this all night. If it wasn't so cold, I'd crank my window open a crevice, so I can let the sound lullaby me to sleep."

"Ma-waugh," Scout agreed.

"Well, there's only one problem with that scenario," Colleen countered.

"What?"

"Didn't you notice? None of the windows have screens on them."

Katherine's eyes grew big. "Glad you told me. I can see me getting up in the middle of the night, half-asleep and cranking the window—"

Colleen chuckled. "And the two terror twins would be sure to get out."

"They're not terror twins," Katherine defended.

Colleen tipped her head back and belted out a loud laugh. "Really? You could have fooled me."

Mum added, "I would call them precocious."

"Yes, Mum, you're right. Scout and Abra are very curious . . . I mean very, very curious," Katherine said.

Colleen reached down and petted Abra. "Is this true?"

"Raw," the Siamese answered, blinking an eye kiss.

Mum began. "It feels so great to be here . . . to be out of the noise of the big city . . . just the three of us for a long weekend. Soon you'll be married Colleen, and the next time we're together like this, Daryl will be here, too."

Colleen laughed. "Don't worry about that, Mum. Daryl gives me my space. There'll be more times like this."

The Siamese startled. Scout swiveled her ears in the direction of the beach. Abra stood up, stretched, and jumped down. The Siamese padded over to the side of the porch facing the water. They began wildly sniffing the air. Scout began digging.

Katherine launched off her chair. "What are you two doing?" Then she realized they were digging at a small hole in the screen, she yelled, "Get away from there."

Scout arched her back; Abra arched hers. "Mir-waugh . . . waugh . . . waugh."

Colleen got up and joined Katherine. "What's wrong? What are they looking at?"

Scout's fur bristled on her back. "Waugh," she cried urgently.

Katherine peered out through the screen at total blackness. "I can't see anything beyond the porch light, and that's not very far."

Mum took the distraction as her opportunity to help herself to the boxed wine. She crept over to the table and filled her tumbler to the top.

75

Someone ran past the cabin, pounding the sand with their feet. A woman yelled a bloodcurdling scream.

The Siamese screeched like banshees.

"The Saints preserve us, who is that?" Mum asked.

"Shhh," Katherine shushed her. "Listen."

The heavy footsteps continued. The woman screamed again, but her words were finally recognizable. "Come back to me."

Katherine and Colleen stood in total shock, both afraid of moving an inch for fear of what would happen next.

Mum broke the ice. "Let's go inside. It's not safe to be out here when you can't see a bloomin' thing."

Katherine snatched Scout around the middle. Scout struggled to be put down. "Oh, no you don't. You're coming inside. Colleen, get Abra."

"That should be an easy task," Colleen said facetiously, chasing down the faster-than-greased-lightning feline. Abra darted out of the room.

"Mum, shut the door," Katherine said, as she dove into the living room.

Colleen continued chasing Abra, down the hallway, into her room. "Got you," she said.

Mum ran for the boxed wine, retrieved it, and then moved in front of the fireplace. "Katz, are there any logs to burn? I'm chilled to the bone."

Katherine noticed that mum hadn't locked the door to the porch. "One second," she said, stepping over and locking the door," then she moved to the fireplace. "It's not a wood-burning fireplace. It has a gas insert. Here let me turn it on." Katherine flipped the switch over the mantel, and a blue fire rose behind a ceramic-imitation log. "When you want to turn it off, just flip the switch again."

"Thanks, love."

Colleen came back in the room. "I've locked Abra up."

Katherine had already set Scout down. "You can let her out. I think they'll be okay now."

Colleen gave an exasperated look and returned to their bedroom to release the excited cat.

Mum suggested, "Katz, love, maybe we should call the police?"

A loud knock rapped on the back door. Katherine startled. "Who is that?"

Colleen said, "Don't answer it."

The person outside was now pounding on the door.

Katherine moved over to see who it was.

Colleen grabbed her by the arm. "The last time you did this, back at that farmhouse from hell, you let Sam Sanders in and he tried to kill us."

"Maybe someone needs help."

"Like that nut case running outside screaming?"

"Yes, exactly. Wait here. I'm going to answer it."

"Where's your Glock?" Colleen asked, worried.

Mum interjected, "Now, there's no need for a handgun, my dear. There're three of us here. We can deal with whoever it is."

"Colleen, we don't need it," Katherine said, opening the door a crack.

A slender woman in her thirties with long, straight black hair, stood outside. "Hello, I'm Kate. I'm staying in the cabin next door."

"And?" Katherine prodded, wanting the woman to hurry up and state her business.

"I'm so sorry, but I've done a really stupid thing. I managed to lock myself out of my cabin."

"Oh, not good," Katherine said, sizing up the situation. She opened the door. "Please, come in. How can I help you?"

Kate looked around. "I apologize for barging in on you at this hour, but I saw your lights on. I also managed to lock my cell phone inside the cabin as well. I was wondering if you could call a locksmith for me."

"Sure, but it's midnight. Would a locksmith be available at this hour?" Katherine asked.

"There's a twenty-four-hour service in Seagull," the woman said, then looked down, embarrassed. "This isn't the first time I've done this. I've called them several times."

"Well, okay. Would you like to come inside? We've got a warm fire burning in the fireplace."

"Yes. Thank you."

Mum said, "Hello, let me introduce you to my daughter, Colleen."

Colleen stood in front of the fireplace and gave Kate a suspicious look.

Kate said, "Pleased to meet you."

"I'm Mum. My name is Maggie, but you can call me Mum. Everyone else does."

"Okay," Kate said. "I'm happy to meet my new neighbors. Are you here long?"

Katherine answered, scrolling through Google sites for Seagull locksmiths. "We're staying until Sunday."

Colleen asked Kate, "Why don't you walk down to the manager's cabin and see if he can help?"

Kate explained, "When I drove up, there weren't any vehicles parked outside, so I'm assuming they haven't gotten back yet from wherever they've been. Have you met them?" Kate inquired curiously.

Mum said, "Yes, when I got here, I met the woman . . . Misty. She gave me the keys. I didn't see him."

"Arlo's a piece of work, I can tell you," Kate said. "I've been here for a little over four months, and each time I run into Misty, she's wearing a fresh black eye."

Mum said, "Did you ask the poor girl about it?"

"I asked her once, and one time only. She came up with this lame excuse that she fell off her porch. I didn't ask her for an excuse the second time."

Colleen asked, "I wonder why she puts up with it?"

Kate shrugged her shoulders. "I don't know what she sees in Arlo. She's in her thirties, and he is at least seventy."

"No accounting for taste," Colleen said.

"Let's be fair, Colleen," Mum advised. "Maybe his wife loves the man for who he is and not for his age."

Colleen scoffed and repeated Mum's words, "Loves the man for who he is. A wife beater!"

Kate said, "I've seen the two of them together, walking hand-in-hand on the beach. He seems devoted to her."

"Maybe she's clumsy and really did fall off the porch," Mum said.

Kate added, "I can say that she takes very good care of him. Arlo had a heart attack several months ago. Before he got ill, he was doing maintenance on the cabins. Misty hired a new guy to take over Arlo's job. He's in his thirties and very flirty. He moved into the last cabin in our row, four doors down from your cabin. I don't mean to gossip, but Misty just bought a brand-new pickup and guess who's driving it?"

Mum said, "The new lad."

"Yep," Kate answered.

Katherine cut in. "Bingo, I've found a locksmith."

"Oh, gosh, I forgot to tell you the one I use is called Seagull locksmiths," Kate apologized.

"Yep, got it," Katherine said, punching in the number. She spoke into the phone and gave the information, then asked Kate, "What's your cabin number?"

"1313."

Katherine did a curious side glance at Colleen, then said into the phone, "1313 Beach Road. When can you be here? Okay, that's fine. We'll look for you then." She disconnected the call and announced, "He'll be here in an hour."

"Oh, that's good. Now if you excuse me, I'll just go sit on my back porch and wait for him."

Colleen suggested, still wary of the woman, "Why don't you sit in your car? Wouldn't that be warmer?"

Kate answered, embarrassed. "I would if it wasn't locked."

"Oh, bad luck," Mum said, pouring another glass from the wine box. "At least take a seat and make yourself comfortable," she motioned toward the loveseat.

"Is that okay? I don't mean to intrude."

Scout and Abra charged into the room, and immediately went over to Kate. They began brushing against her.

Kate gushed, "I can't take it," she said, clutching her heart. "They are the most . . . drop-dead gorgeous . . . Siamese I've ever seen."

Katherine beamed. "Thank you. You must be a cat person."

"How can you tell?"

"Because, Scout and Abra don't take kindly to strangers."

"I'm flattered," Kate said, reaching down to pet both cats.

Colleen bluntly asked, "Kate, we heard a woman run past our cabin. She was screaming her head off. Was that you?"

Kate's eyes grew wide. She hesitated for a moment, then explained, "I know that you're going to think I'm totally out of my mind, but that wasn't a woman—"

Mum said, "Sounded like a woman."

Colleen added sarcastically, "It certainly wasn't a seagull doing a voice impression of a screaming woman."

Kate said slowly, "It wasn't me. I'm afraid you've heard the phantom voice of a woman long-dead."

"A spirit?" Colleen asked excitedly.

Kate nodded.

"Pause. Hold that thought," Katherine said to Kate. "Let me pour you a glass a wine."

"Yes, I'd love some."

Katherine walked over to the boxed wine, hit the tap and poured a glass. Returning to Kate, she handed her the glass. "You said a long time? What did you mean?"

Kate took the goblet and drank several sips. "I meant over eighty years."

Colleen finally sat down in a chair across from Kate. "You said 'phantom voice.' Has anyone ever seen this spirit?"

"Oh, yeah, it's common knowledge. There're several people in town who would swear they saw her walking on the beach."

Katherine commented, "Interesting. The voice was as clear as day. My cats heard her, too. In fact, while we were sitting out on the porch, my cats were the ones that alerted us to someone running past our cabin."

Scout and Abra had lost interest in the newcomer, and had taken spots in front of the fireplace.

"Have you ever heard the Seagull legend?" Kate asked.

"No, can't say I have," Katherine answered.

Colleen shook her head, "We're not from around here."

Kate took another sip, and began, "Back in the thirties, a man and woman, husband and wife, had a cabin on this beach. The woman was from a rich family; the man was from a poor one. He also had a criminal background. They truly loved each other, well, that's at least what the townspeople say, but the couple fought like cats and dogs," Kate said, then paused for several seconds. She continued, "And, they drank like fish! One night they had too much to drink, and got into an argument. She accused him of cheating on her. He denied it. She ran out of the house, and he chased after her, but he didn't get far."

"What happened?" Colleen asked.

"He tripped over a kerosene lantern. They were not the tidiest of people, and the contents of the house quickly caught on fire. The house exploded in flames."

Mum made of a sign of the cross. "'Twas terrible."

Kate nodded. "The fire department was too late, and the house burned to the ground."

Colleen said knowingly, "That's typical of a haunting, especially the part of leaving this world before you're ready. Plus, dying so tragically. I assume it was the husband who died in the fire?"

"Yes, that's it in a nutshell. At first, the fire chief thought she had died as well, but later she was found on the beach babbling like a crazy woman."

Katherine asked, "Let me get the facts straight. The husband died, the wife survived. What happened to her?"

"Oh, she spent a few years at an insane asylum—"

Colleen interrupted, "Another key ingredient to a haunting. The woman went daft and forever walks the moors searching for Heathcliff."

Katherine chuckled. "I think Colleen means the beach and not the moors."

Kate laughed. "I've read *Wuthering Heights*. I loved it."

"Me, too," Katherine added.

Kate finished. "She was released and died a few years later. To make ends meet, she'd walk the beach, picking up bits of debris that she'd make into necklaces and sell to tourists."

Colleen asked, "I thought you said she came from a wealthy family."

"They disowned her when she married her husband."

"Wow, what kind of parents do that?" Katherine asked, rolling her eyes.

"To finish the legend," Kate said, yawning, "She died of a broken heart. Two years to the date of the fire, her body was found not far from our cabins. She was nude and lying face-down in the surf."

Mum gulped down the rest of her glass. "Lovely," she slurred.

Colleen jumped out of her chair. "Mum, hand me your glass."

"Whatever for, dear? It's just apple juice."

Colleen sniffed the drink. "Bloody hell, Mum. How much have you drank?"

"A wee bit."

Kate looked surprised.

Katherine whispered, "Mum had a drinking problem."

"I heard that," Mum protested. She got up from her chair and stomped to her room. "I'd much rather be in me room . . . alone . . . then out here with a bunch of harpies. Good night." She slammed the door.

"Raw," Abra cried, running her paw over her ear.

Katherine consoled. "It's okay, darlings. Go back to your heat basking."

"Fine," Colleen shouted after her, then she looked at Kate. "I'm sorry you had to witness that."

Kate got up. "Ladies, I really must wait for the locksmith."

Katherine offered, "But you can stay here until he gets here."

"I just want to make sure he doesn't leave when I'm not out there . . . waiting."

"Well, okay, then, but I insist you wear a coat."

"Yes, that would be nice. It's freezing outside."

Katherine took her pea jacket off the coat rack and handed it to Kate. "You can return it tomorrow."

"Thank you ever so much," Kate said, opening the back door.

Katherine said, "Wait, Kate, I have a quick question. What were the names of the couple, so I can Google them."

"Her name was Madeline—"

Colleen walked over, "Madeline? The flier I picked up at the gas station said the spirit's name is Diana?"

"Oh, no, that's a different ghost. Similar history, but Madeline only appears when a murder is going to be committed."

"Seriously?" Colleen quizzed.

Kate nodded. "The ghost hasn't appeared since a murder on the beach two years ago."

"But you called her Seagull's own."

"Whenever someone in town or on the beach is going to be murdered, Madeline appears. Now, if you'll excuse me, I must really go. Thanks so much for everything," she said, leaving. "Bye now."

Katherine closed the door, and leaned the security bar underneath the door handle. Jake had insisted she bring it as a special precaution so no one would break in.

Colleen joked, "I hate to tell you this, Katz. But a spirit can walk through doors."

"Hush, you. I'll never get any sleep," Katherine said with a twinkle in her eye.

"I'm calling it a day," Colleen said, heading for their bedroom. "Oh, Katz, the cats seem to be fine out here. Why don't we move their litterbox out here, so they don't wake us up with their shenanigans?"

Katherine asked the cats, "Is that okay with you?"

"Ma-waugh," Scout answered, now half-asleep on the hearth.

"Well, okay, we can try it," Katherine said, reaching over and turning off the switch to the gas fireplace. "You girls be good."

Chapter Seven

Late Thursday Night at Cabin One

How Long has This Been Goin' On?

Misty nervously paced back and forth on the sandy yard outside her cabin, and waited for Josh to return her call. Arlo had found out they were having an affair, and she had to warn her lover. She'd texted and called him several times, but he didn't answer. She tried him again. "Answer your stupid phone," she said anxiously.

Misty replayed in her mind what happened the day before, when Arlo came back from the hardware store. She was in Cabin Five making up one of the bunk beds. Arlo came in, fixed the toilet, and then left. She thought it was odd that he didn't speak to her the entire time he was in the cabin. She finished cleaning around noon, then returned to the office. Sitting behind the desk, she checked her email. She was thrilled that cabins two through five were booked into July. She smiled.

Arlo walked in with a murderous look, Misty remembered.

"Better wipe that grin off your face," he said.

"What's wrong?" she asked apprehensively.

91

"This morning when I was at the hardware store, Joe had something interesting to tell me."

"By the look on your face, it must have been a good one," she scoffed.

"He told me he caught you and Josh making out. How long has this been goin' on?"

"That's ridiculous. Joe's a liar."

"Don't try and weasel your way out of this. I trust my friend over you any day."

"Thanks for your vote of confidence," Misty said, getting up.

Arlo reached across the desk and pushed her back into her chair. "If you know what's good for you, you'd better stay out of my way."

"What are you talking about?"

Arlo yanked a key off the key holder on the wall. "I'm moving into Cabin Six." He went into the bedroom and returned a few minutes later with a suitcase.

Misty demanded, "Give me my Cherokee keys back?"

"No way. You get the new truck back from lover boy—"

"He's not my lover boy," she protested. "Joe's out of his mind."

"I don't know what possessed me to let you hire an ex-con."

"Arlo, I need my keys," she pleaded. "Give them to me!"

"Drive my truck," Arlo said with a smirk.

"The battery is dead!"

"Have lover boy jump start it. He seems to be good at that sort of thing. He's already jump-started you."

After that argument, Arlo had stormed out of the cabin and driven off in her Cherokee, leaving her stranded at the cabins without a vehicle.

Around dinner time, Misty realized Arlo had not taken his meds with him when he left. She gathered the prescription bottles and walked to Cabin Six. Arlo wasn't there, and when she looked behind the cabin at the parking lot, her Cherokee wasn't there either. Only the disabled pickup remained.

She called Arlo several times, but each time her call was directed to his voicemail.

The next day, Arlo was nowhere to be found. She called a number of his friends, but none of them had seen him. She hesitated to call big-mouth Joe, and when she did, her call rang and rang. She surmised that Arlo and Joe had gone to their favorite casino and had gambled the night away. They probably got drunk and were sleeping it off.

Misty was very busy on Thursday and didn't have time to keep walking to Cabin Six to see if Arlo had returned. She stayed up until eleven, then went to bed. She had just gotten to sleep, when she heard the key turn in the back door. Arlo barged in and dragged her out of bed. He started accusing her of all sorts of things. Most of the accusations were false, such as she'd been cheating with men for years, which was ridiculous because she'd been loyal to Arlo until Josh.

When Arlo got to the part about Josh, she couldn't lie. Worn down by the argument, she confessed. She hoped it would make her feel better, but it didn't.

Arlo went into a rage and threatened to kill Josh. He ran out of the cabin and took the dune path in front of the cabins. Misty ran after him. Instinctively, she knew he was heading for Josh's cabin, which didn't make sense because she'd already told him Josh wouldn't be back until late Friday night. She thought, *if only Arlo would fall down the dune and break his neck. Then, his death would purely be an accident.*

She'd caught up with Arlo as he was turning the manager's key in Josh's door. "I told you already. He's not coming back until tomorrow night. Can we talk this through?"

Arlo stopped and glared at her.

"Say something? Where have you been?" Misty asked angrily. "I've been worried sick about you."

"Don't you fret about me. You better worry about what I'm going to do to lover boy."

"What do you mean?"

"It's simple. I'm going to break his neck."

"Arlo, please, I beg of you. Don't kill him. I'll call it off. I'll break up with him and tell him to leave. You'll never see him again. I promise. I made a terrible mistake. Please, come back home with me."

Arlo brushed past her.

"Now where are you going?"

Arlo didn't answer. He headed to Cabin Six, opened the side door and walked in.

Misty ran after him. "Arlo, I need my keys. I have supplies to pick up tomorrow."

Arlo reached into his pocket and pulled out her keys. He threw them at her. "Have fun hitching a ride to Gary," he fumed.

"Gary? What are you talking about?"

"I drove it to the Bigmart and left it there, but I'm not telling you where I parked it. Have some more fun finding it in their busy parking lot."

"You lie. You didn't do something so stupid. If you did, how did you get back here?"

Arlo laughed. "My buddy Joe picked me up."

"Damn you," Misty cursed.

"Oh, and another thing, I'm going to call Sheriff Earle and tell him Josh stole my truck. How do you like those apples?" he said, slamming the door.

"I hate you," Misty yelled through the closed door. She walked to the service road behind the cabins. She stopped several times to call Josh, but he didn't pick up. Finally, she left a voicemail and told him not to return until Monday. She hoped by then Arlo would have calmed down. When she got back to her cabin, she turned to see who was driving down the lane. Her heart skipped a beat. Josh pulled up in the new Sierra.

Josh parked, opened his door and stepped out. Misty met him on the sidewalk.

Josh yanked Misty in an embrace, but when he tried to kiss her, she turned her face. "Hey, what's the matter with you? Didn't you miss me?" he asked, dejected.

"What are you doing here? I thought you weren't coming back until Friday."

Josh ignored the question. "That's a fine welcome," he said, pushing her away. "I've been bustin' my chops getting that drug you wanted to off your husband."

"Shhh," Misty said. "Voices carry. Someone might hear you."

"What are you doing outside this late at night? What's up?"

"Look, Josh, Arlo knows about us. He freaked out."

"Where is he?" Josh asked, suddenly concerned. He didn't want to fight Arlo, who was strong as an ox.

"He said he was going to kill you. He ran off to your cabin, but I chased him down and said you weren't there."

"You didn't answer my question. Where is he now?" Josh said, looking around.

"He moved into Cabin Six."

"Great. Right next to mine. That sucks."

"Big time."

Josh caught her by the arm and put his hand over her mouth. "Someone's walking up the sidewalk next door."

Misty broke free. "It's Kate," she whispered. "Come inside. We don't want her to see us."

They ducked into the manager's cabin.

Josh said, "I don't think she saw us, but I'd better move the truck."

"I don't think it's safe for you to go to your cabin. I want you to stay at the Seagull Inn until Monday."

"Monday. Seagull Inn? Do I look like I have money?"

"I can give you some."

Josh shrugged the offer off. "I don't want your money. I'll drive down to the truck stop and sleep in the truck."

Misty said, "And, that's another thing, Arlo wants the truck back. He said he was calling the sheriff and telling him that you stole it."

"I ain't afraid of no country bumpkin sheriff."

"Josh, you have to give it back."

"Well, I can't."

"Why?"

"I've got things to do."

Misty didn't ask him what kind of things he had to do. She began to cry.

Josh took her in his arms. "It's gonna be okay," he said tenderly.

They kissed a long, passionate kiss, then Josh left.

"I'll see you tomorrow," he called from the side door.

"No, don't come back until I tell you to. I have to work this thing out with Arlo."

Josh didn't answer but got in the truck, fired up the engine, and took off.

Chapter Eight

Friday Morning

Back at the Erie Diner

The Erie diner was buzzing with its usual morning crowd, who were mostly men. Cushioned-seated booths lined three of the walls. In the center was a number of tables pushed up against each other to form a long table. The set-up was similar on the right-hand and left-hand sides. The tables were not reserved, but there was an understanding in Erie that you sat at the table with your group mostly comprised of the town gossips. The peak period of the "gossip, general news, and downright lies" was between five and nine a.m. The far-left table was the ball-cap table, and was frequented by construction, maintenance, and HVAC workers. Jake's dad Johnny and his Uncle Cokey sat at this table. Whenever Jake would come to the restaurant, he'd join them at the ball-cap table. His friends at the table affectionately called him Professor Jake. The far-right table was where the farmers sat with their caps advertising the latest corn hybrid or the name of a feed store outside the town limits. The center table was frequented by retired men from all sorts of professions.

This became known as the liars' table based on the frequency of downright tall tales that were spun by this group of very imaginative men.

By nine a.m. the breakfast crowd would clear out. Men would settle their checks, go outside, jump in their pickups, and either go home or to work. Servers would divide and move the tables to accommodate the lunch crowd. If you were a woman in Erie, and you didn't want to be talked about, you wouldn't go to the diner until lunch time.

The dynamics of the diner never changed.

At seven, in the morning, James John, known around town as Jimbo, arrived. He walked in the diner to find two long tables filled with patrons, but the liars' table was empty. He was dismayed that his cohorts hadn't shown up yet. He had some news that would blow their minds. He took a seat, grabbed the empty coffee cup that was sitting on the table, and tapped it on the table. That was his way of ordering coffee.

Ruby, a good-hearted widow in her forties, with curly, prematurely gray hair, grabbed a fresh pot and headed to Jimbo.

"Good mornin', Ruby girl," Jimbo greeted. "How's business?"

Ruby scoffed, "Been the same as it's always been."

Jimbo teased, "You should know. Didn't ya start workin' here in 1950?"

"Ain't been here that long," she said with one hand on her hip. "Keep that up, Mister, and you'll find a fly in your eggs."

Jimbo roared with laughter. "Ah, you know I love ya, Ruby."

"Yeah, right," Ruby answered, heading to the next customer.

Jimbo fidgeted at the table. He sipped his coffee and checked out newcomers as they came in. After ten minutes, he was thrilled when his two friends, Clarence and Buster, arrived. The two men walked into the restaurant and greeted everyone they knew with a loud hello, the word reverberating off the metal-clad diner walls.

"Ruby," Jimbo called. "Bring that coffee pot over."

"Just a sec, buddy. Can't ya see I'm busy?" She went over to another table and poured coffee, took their orders, then came back over to Jimbo. "What are you liars gonna be talkin' about today?" she asked with a big smile.

"I ain't sayin'," Jimbo said, winking.

Ruby poured coffee in the newcomer's cups, then topped off Jimbo's. "I guess I'll find out soon enough. Word travels fast around here." She moved off to wait on another customer.

Jimbo began, "I've got news that will make your teeth drop."

"Out with it," Clarence said.

"It's a good one," Jimbo said.

"Well, tell it," Buster insisted.

"You know how I had to go to Rensselaer yesterday?"

"Yeah, to see your daughter," Clarence answered, then prodded, "And?"

"I took my daughter and my son-in-law to this great BBQ place. If you haven't been there you really need to go," Jimbo said.

"I think I've been there. Lou's Place, right?"

"Yep, that's it. I had a stack of ribs oozing with Lou's brand of BBQ sauce, a mound of special seasoned French fries, and a bowl of coleslaw that had just the right amount of celery seeds and sugar in it."

"Get to the point? What's your juicy gossip?" Buster asked.

"I walked in and there sittin' in the back was Stevie Sanders."

Ruby caught the name Stevie Sanders and walked over to the table. Any topic relating to one of the Sanders boys was hot news. The Sanders dated way back in Erie's history. Great Grandpa Sanders was a bootlegger; his son's son, now deceased, was a kingpin of criminal activity. Stevie was a less-frequent topic because he had gone clean, so there wasn't much to talk about him, until . . .

"What was he doing there?" Ruby asked nosily.

A crowd of men walked in the diner, laughing at something they'd been talking about in the parking lot. They joined the three men at the liars' table.

Clarence said, "Sit down, fellahs. Jimbo has a good one to tell ya."

In unison, the men asked for coffee, but Ruby didn't move to get it. "Keep talkin'," she said to Jimbo.

Jimbo filled them in. "I was in Rensselaer last night at that BBQ place — Lou's Place. I spotted Stevie Sanders sittin' at a table with a woman from Erie."

"That's not a scoop," Clarence said.

"Let me finish."

Buster elbowed Jimbo on the arm, "Who was she?"

"Jake Cokenberger's wife."

"No way!" the men said, shocked.

Clarence added his two cents. "Word is all over town that Stevie hasn't dated anyone since he got out of the pen because he's in love with Jake's wife."

"Yeah, you're right," one of the newcomers reflected. "He even bought the house next to hers."

Another one added, "That's suspicious. Stevie would know the whereabouts of Jake at all times, then you know . . ." He didn't finish the comment, but the group at the table got the gist of what he'd said.

"Her name is Katherine," Buster said. "Nice lady. It couldn't have been her. She's nuts over her husband."

"You callin' me a liar? It was her," Jimbo begged to differ. "Since I had my cataracts removed, I can see clear as a sunny day."

"What did she look like?"

"She had long black hair and beautiful green eyes."

"How the heck did you see the color of her eyes?"

"She had this emerald green blouse on, and the lighting in the restaurant was such, that when she glanced at me, just one time, I could see how green her eyes were."

"You've got it wrong. Katherine Cokenberger has short black hair," Buster corrected.

"I know it was her."

"Maybe she was wearing a wig," Clarence said.

"A wig. Don't be ridiculous!" a man at the far end said.

"As a disguise. She didn't want anybody to recognize her."

"In Rensselaer? That's miles from here. Takes a good hour to drive it. What are the odds that three people from Erie would be there at the same time?"

"Just sayin," Jimbo defended. "Three from Erie. Stevie, Jake's wife, and me."

"Yeah, how many people from Erie hang out there?" Clarence asked.

"I was there," Jimbo said adamantly. "I tell you it was Jake's wife."

"Can we get some service here?" a man sitting in a booth, called over to Ruby.

"Yes, coming," she said, heading to the other customer.

One of the ball-capped men sitting next to the liars' table leaned over and asked Jimbo, "Are you sure about that? I wouldn't want to cross the Cokenberger clan. Or the Sanders bunch. If Stevie finds out you're talkin' about him, you better hide."

Jimbo put up his hand. "Scout's honor, Ben! I saw it with my own two eyes."

Ben turned in his chair and told the man on his left who told the next man. The information was hot. The word spread like a children's telephone game. In less than five minutes, the entire diner was buzzing with the news: Stevie Sanders was having an affair with Katherine Cokenberger.

Chapter Nine

Friday Morning at the Seagull Cabin Three

Scout and Abra sat side-by-side on the bedroom's windowsill and were looking intently at something outside. Scout's tail was twitching; Abra's was flipping back and forth.

"At-at-at-at-at!" Scout clucked.

Katherine jumped out of bed. "What's going on?" she said in a low voice, so as to not disturb Colleen, who was still asleep.

"How did you two get in here?" The bedroom door was standing wide-open. "What are you looking at?" she asked, joining them at the window. She tugged the curtains open and looked outside. A large seagull was perched on the other side of the window. When the bird saw the human, it began pecking on the glass. "That's the biggest gull I've ever seen."

Colleen moaned from the top bunk, "What's that noise? Make it stop."

The seagull squawked and continued pecking on the glass.

Scout reared up and drummed the window with her front paws.

"What time is it?" Katherine said to the lump on the top bunk.

"I don't care," Colleen said, pulling the comforter over her head.

Katherine grabbed her cell phone off the charger and checked the time. "Oh, my, it's nine o'clock. Doesn't Mum have something planned for us this morning?"

Colleen threw the covers off. "You're right. We're supposed to go to the spa today."

"There's a spa at the Dunes State Park?" Katherine asked incredulously.

Colleen laughed. "There's one in Michigan City. Supposedly, it's the best spa in the Midwest."

"Okay, I vote the gal on the lower bunk gets the bathroom first." Katherine ran out of the room.

"Cheater," Colleen called.

The seagull gave a final squawk and flew away.

Colleen climbed the bunk's ladder to the floor, then threw on her robe. She walked into the small kitchen. Mum was sitting at the table, drinking a cup of tea. "Good morning. How are you this morning?"

"Not so good," Mum answered.

"What's wrong?"

"I've got a bit of a headache. Would you girls mind if I don't go to the spa with you this morning."

Colleen sat down across from her mother. "I know why you have the headache," she said knowingly.

"I don't need a lecture, dearie."

"If you don't go with us, what are you going to do today?"

"Just putter about the cabin, sit on the porch and read."

Katherine came into the kitchen with her hair lathered up with shampoo.

"The Saints preserve us. What happened to you?" Mum asked.

"I was halfway through my shower, when the hot water gave out."

Mum suggested. "Sounds like a problem with the water heater. Find me a match and I'll go light it."

Colleen and Katherine said in unison. "No, that won't be necessary." Neither one of them trusted Mum to know what she was doing, and feared she'd blow the place up.

Katherine asked, "Do you have the manager's card?"

Mum answered, "It's on the refrigerator. It has a magnet of a fish on it."

Katherine moved over and extracted the business card. She punched in the number on her phone. While the phone rang, she asked, "Mum, what's his name again? It just has a first initial here."

"I never met the man. Ask for Misty."

Katherine mouthed the word *thanks*, then spoke into the phone. "May I speak to the manager, please? Oh, he's not at home. I want to report a problem in Cabin Three. Yes, a problem. There's no hot water," she complained. "Yes, today would be good, but tell him to not use his key. I have two cats and I don't want them to get out. Yes, yes. Two cats. I paid a pet deposit when I booked the room, remember? Of course, you remember. I didn't mean to suggest otherwise. Okay, I'll be here to meet him. Noon, you said. Yes, that's great. Thanks," she said, hanging up.

"She was rather testy," Katherine commented. When Colleen and Mum didn't answer, she said, "I won't be able to go to the spa with you two. I have to be here at noon to let in the maintenance man."

"Mum's not going with us today," Colleen said.

"Why?"

"I can wait for him," Mum offered.

"That works, but why aren't you going to the spa with us?"

"Got a wee bit of a headache."

Colleen smirked. "Katz, what are you going to do about your hair?"

"I thought I'd jump in the lake and wash it there. The water would probably be warmer."

Mum rose from her chair, "Come here, Katz. Put your head over the sink. I'll use bottled water to wash it out."

"Yeah, it's so short, it shouldn't take too much," Colleen kidded.

"Okay, carrot top, enough with my short hair," Katherine said.

Colleen covered her face to conceal a giggle.

*   *   *

Later in the afternoon, Katherine and Colleen drove back from the spa, and were several miles from the cabin, when a deputy sheriff's vehicle, with its siren wailing and red lights flashing, passed them.

Katherine said, "Wow, he came out of nowhere. He must be doing ninety."

In a few minutes, another deputy vehicle passed them.

Both vehicles turned onto Beach Road.

Colleen asked apprehensively, "Katz, isn't that our road?"

"Yeah, that's it. I wonder what's going on."

"It's pretty remote back there. Step on the gas, so we get to the cabin sooner. I have a psychic feeling that Mum is in trouble."

Katherine floored the accelerator and sped down the curvy road. She overshot her lane and nearly hit a firetruck head-on.

Colleen screamed. "Look out!"

Katherine swerved to the right to avoid hitting it. She braked and put the SUV in park.

The driver of the fire truck stopped. He powered his window down; Katherine did the same.

"What's your hurry? You drive like you're running out of a house on fire," he laughed loudly.

Katherine made an annoyed face, and drove off. Driving into the cabin's lane, she noticed the two deputy vehicles were parked in back of Cabin Three.

"This can't be good," Colleen said. "Stop the car. I have to see if Mum is all right."

Katherine drove around the vehicles and parked.

The deputies were chatting to each other outside the back door.

Katherine ran to them. "What happened?"

They stopped talking and looked at Katherine suspiciously.

Colleen ran up. "I'm the daughter. Is my mother okay?"

The first deputy, with an over-sized mustache, said, "You need to tell your mother to stop playing with matches."

"Why? What's going on?" Katherine asked.

"She tried to light a pilotless water heater, and set off a series of events that nearly caught the cabin on fire."

"Is she okay?" Colleen asked.

"Yes, she's inside." Colleen flew into the cabin.

Katherine lingered behind for a few seconds. "So, I'm curious, why are you two here?"

"Just doing our job," the other one said. "Good day, ma'am," he said, walking to his vehicle. The other deputy got into his.

Katherine didn't stay to watch them leave. She hurried into the cabin. She covered her nose. The acrid smell of smoke was sickening. Someone had placed a box fan in the front living room window, but it wasn't doing a very good job of getting rid of the smell.

Colleen joined Mum at the table.

"Girls, I'm fine. Don't worry," Mum said nervously.

"What happened?"

"That manager eejit didn't show up, so I took matters in me own hands. How hard can it be to light a water heater?"

Katherine looked up at the ceiling and rolled her eyes. "Where are the cats?"

"I put them in your bedroom. Oh, one of the handsome lads from the fire department checked on them. He said they were fine, but he opened the window to freshen the room."

Katherine and Colleen shouted at the same time. "There're no screens on the windows!"

Katherine rushed into the bedroom. No cats. She flattened down on the floor and looked underneath the bunk bed. Still no cats. She called them, "Scout. Abra." The cats didn't answer. Then she yelled at the top of her lungs. "They got outside."

Colleen ran in. "Katz, we'll find them. I'll help."

Mum called from the kitchen table, "I'll help, too."

Katherine barked, "You've done enough for the day. Stay out of it."

Katherine bolted out of the cabin and walked the perimeter of the house. Colleen headed in the opposite direction. When they met, Katherine became frantic. "Where could they go?"

"Surely, they wouldn't wander off in that woods over there."

Katherine glanced over at a clump of closely planted trees nestled in overgrown weeds. "That would be a nightmare."

Colleen walked to the edge of the property and peered over the edge of the sand dune. "Katz, come over here. What's that on the beach?"

"Where?" Katherine asked, joining her.

"There, right there," she pointed anxiously.

"It's the cats." Katherine didn't waste time backtracking to the path to the beach. She jumped over the sand dune, slipped, and fell on her back. She slid down the slope until her fall was stopped by a large piece of driftwood. Picking herself up, she ran to the Siamese.

Abra was digging in the sand, and making a series of proud muttering sounds. Scout seemed poised to jump in the lake. She swiveled her head toward Katherine, then looked at the lake.

Katherine coaxed. "Scout, no . . . no . . . come to mommy. Treat! Treat!"

Scout ignored her and jumped into the surf. She began paddling away.

Colleen, taking the easier route, ran up. "I'm not used to this back-to-nature stuff," she complained.

"Take Abra," Katherine said. "I'll get Scout."

"Where is she?"

"She jumped in the darn lake."

"Can she swim?"

"Apparently," Katherine said, exasperated.

Colleen picked up Abra, and gazed down at what Abra had been digging. With one hand she took hold of the cat, and with the other one, she picked up a leather wallet.

117

She stuck it in her jeans' front pocket. She trod back to the cabin with Abra tucked under her arm. The Siamese shrieked like she was being tortured, and wriggled the entire way.

"Quit it!" Colleen said, "Stop squirming."

Meanwhile, Katherine spotted Scout's head bobbing in the water about ten feet from the shore. The Siamese had something in her mouth.

Katherine waded in, grabbed the wet cat, and held her close. "What do you think you're doing? You gave your mommy a heart attack." Then she noticed what was in Scout's mouth — a very dead fish.

"Ew, drop it," Katherine ordered.

Scout growled.

Katherine massaged her jaw.

Scout bit harder into the fish.

At her wit's end, Katherine said, "You win. Just take it." She held Scout close and trudged back to the cabin. "Oh my, you smell. I know a very stinky Siamese that's getting a bath."

"No-waugh," Scout complained in a muffled voice.

Entering the cabin, Katherine took Scout to the bathroom and closed the door. Colleen knocked on the door and said, "I locked Abra in our bedroom. What's that god-awful smell?"

"Scout caught a fish and won't let me have it. Hey, I'll be out in a minute. Put the kettle on."

"I'm on it," Colleen said, walking away.

A very guilty Mum sat at the table and fidgeted with her tumbler. "I guess I put me foot in it. I was only trying to help."

"Mum, Katz is very annoyed at you. Maybe you should keep a low profile for a bit."

"Maybe I should go home," Mum said sadly.

"I didn't mean that. Just chill for a bit. What did Katz do with that manager card? I'm calling the clown right now."

Someone knocked on the door.

Mum ignored the knock and said, "I told the firemen what happened."

Colleen moved to open the door. "Don't bother to get up. I'll get it. It's probably that idiot here to fix the water heater." She opened the door. Kate stood outside.

"I don't mean to be nosy, but why was the fire department here?" she asked.

"Come in," Colleen offered. "We're in the kitchen."

"Oh, okay," Kate said, following Colleen.

Kate said hello to Mum. "I was just asking your daughter why the fire department was here."

Mum answered glumly, "I tried to light the blasted water heater with a wad of paper, and the paper fell out of me hands, and caught the throw rug on fire."

Kate scrunched up her face. "Oh, not good. What's wrong with the water heater?"

Colleen answered. "We called the manager and he hasn't come to fix it. We don't have any hot water."

"Hey, I can fix that. It's probably the same model that I have in my cabin. The newer models have electronic ignitions. It's an easy thing to do, but there's a trick to it. Do you mind if I have a go at it?"

Colleen said, "Knock yourself out. The water heater is in that little room next to the bat room."

"Bat room? Where's that?"

Mum answered, "The rest room."

"Oh, okay." Kate left the room.

A minute later, Katherine walked in the kitchen, holding a very unhappy Siamese wrapped in a Turkish towel. "Did I hear someone come in?"

Colleen said, "It's Kate. She's fixing the water heater."

"You've got to be kidding me," Katherine said.

Mum said, "Oh, no worries, love. She knows how to do it."

Katherine threw her a dirty look, then asked Colleen, "I have a favor to ask. Can you hold Scout while I get rid of the f-i-s-h?" she spelled.

"It really stinks," Colleen complained.

"Yep."

"Okay, hand me the fisherwoman."

"Waugh," Scout protested.

"Is there a reason why she's still in a towel?"

Katherine glared at her friend. "Because I had to wash her in cold water, and I don't want her to freeze to death."

"Okay! Okay! Don't shoot me."

Katherine grabbed a roll of paper towels and headed back to the bathroom. She picked up the dead fish, wrapped it and carried it out of the cabin. She moved over

121

to the wooded area and threw it as hard as she could into a clump of trees. Then she returned to the kitchen. Kate was explaining to Mum and Colleen that she'd fixed the water heater.

"Yay," Colleen said.

"Hi, Kate. Thanks so much for fixing it," Katherine said. "I wouldn't have a clue how to do it." She almost told the story about what happened on her wedding day, when Mum's son, Jacky, had thrown a cigarette into a pile of oily rags, which blew up the water heater at the pink mansion, but she decided against it.

"It's something I figured out how to do. I'd much rather repair something myself, than put in a call for maintenance," Kate criticized.

"Why?" Colleen asked.

"Because the owner is a dirty old man. He makes crude comments to me. I don't want him anywhere near me."

"I thought you said there was a new guy that did maintenance?" Katherine asked.

"He's never around."

Katherine added, "Maybe I should call Misty and cancel our request."

Kate shook her head. "I wouldn't bother. It doesn't look like anyone is home."

"I'm making tea, Kate. Would you care for a cup?" Colleen offered.

"No, thanks. Listen, I didn't come over to nose about the fire. I came over to invite the three of you to a steak dinner."

Mum said, "This place is so desolate. I didn't know there was a steakhouse nearby."

Kate laughed. "I'm grilling the steaks."

Colleen said, "Yum, that sounds delicious."

"Don't make a fuss on our account," Mum said.

"Oh, there's no fuss at all," Kate assured.

Katherine asked, "Is there anything you want us to bring?"

"Maybe, if it's not too much trouble, you can bring side salads."

"Sure," Katherine said. "I can make coleslaw, that is, if you can point me to the closest grocery store."

"There's a store up the road."

"I didn't notice it driving here."

"Oh, it's easy to find. When you get to the main highway, turn left. You won't miss it. It's called the Seagull 24/7."

Katherine chuckled. "Is everything named Seagull around these parts?"

Kate laughed, "Pretty much. Anyway, we can have a picnic on the beach. Eat steaks, and—"

Mum interrupted, "Talk a bit of treason. We'd love to come, but won't it be too cold?"

Kate answered, "I checked my weather app. It's not supposed to be as cold out as it was last night. Just dress warmly."

"Let us know what else we can do," Katherine said.

"Sure," Kate said, leaving. "You can do me a big favor. Before you head down to the beach, stop by my cabin and help me carry the food. I'll grill steaks at seven, then we can go down."

"Of course, we'll do that," Katherine said, then asked, "Shouldn't we build a campfire?"

Mum offered, tongue-in-check, "I can light a match."

Katherine glowered at her. "Mum, don't go there."

Kate said, "I've got one of those portable firepits. My uncle said he'd come by and move it to the beach. He'll start the fire. Okay, then. I have to get going."

"I'll show you out," Katherine said.

Kate walked to the door and stopped. "If you guys need anything while you're here, please promise you'll ask me. I'm more than happy to help."

"Great, and thanks again for fixing the water heater."

"No problem," Kate said, walking out the door.

*   *   *

Later that evening, Katherine, Colleen and Mum walked to Cabin Two. Kate was standing on her side porch, grilling the steaks on a small portable grill. "Hello, ladies. Tell me how you want your steaks cooked?"

Katherine said, "Medium, thanks."

"Medium well," Colleen said.

Mum added, "Medium rare, so rare you'd think it would jump off the grill and moo."

Colleen brought up her hand to her mouth to stifle a laugh.

Kate laughed.

Katherine wasn't amused. She was still annoyed with Mum for letting the cats out. She thought, *Jake was right. She is a magnet for trouble. Maybe I shouldn't tell him what happened until I get home. He'll probably flip.*

When the steaks were finished, Kate placed them on a metal steak plate, set on a wood base. Colleen carried a store-bought strawberry strudel while Katherine held a bowl of coleslaw.

Kate handed Mum two steak plates. "Can you take these? Just remember your steak is the one in your left hand. You know, the one that mooed."

Mum smiled.

Kate handed Colleen the third plate. "Ladies, I'll join you on the beach. I have to fetch the baked beans I made."

Katherine, Colleen, and Mum walked down the lake access road to the beach. Immediately they were drawn to the idyllic scene of the blazing firepit. Four blankets flanked it.

Kate had thought of everything. A cooler contained soft drinks. She'd placed condiments and silverware in a lidded-metal box. A piece of plywood served as a place for the bowls of food.

"I love this," Colleen gushed.

Katherine smiled, finally letting go of her anger for Mum. She placed the bowl of coleslaw on the board.

Kate walked up, juggling her steak plate and a bowl of baked beans. She set the bowl down next to the slaw. "Okay, everyone dive in. Steak knives are in the bucket. Oh, and, some steak sauce."

Katherine grabbed a knife and cut the first piece of her steak. Tasting it, she said, "Oh, my. This is delicious."

Kate grinned. "You won't believe where I got the steaks."

Mum said merrily, "You went out and found yourself a cow."

"It's kind of a long story, but I'll give you the *Reader's Digest* version."

"Shoot," Colleen said.

"Every month I do volunteer work at the penitentiary."

"Where?" Colleen asked.

"Michigan City."

"Oh, we were just there," Katherine piped in. "I mean we weren't at the prison, but—"

Colleen cut her off. "What kind of volunteer work do you do?"

"I'm an accountant. A CPA."

"Okay, but are you talking about preparing the taxes for the guards or the prisoners?"

"Actually, the prisoners."

"Why would they need help with their taxes? I thought prisoners don't pay taxes."

Kate said between bites, "Prisoners are required to work, but don't make much income. Most don't make enough to file taxes. Besides, I only offer my services to those prisoners who have families in need at home."

"How do you know who those people are?" Colleen asked.

"The warden gives me a list of model prisoners who have a wife or significant other and kids back home. The prisoners are doing their time, so they can get back to them."

"That's sweet," Katherine said. She didn't mention that she did charity work as well. In fact, she didn't want to talk about her status as a millionaire. She'd found that little tidbit of intel changed people's attitude toward her.

She had just wanted a nice, quiet getaway, which was turning out to be far from quiet.

Colleen asked, "So, where did the steaks come from?"

"I left that part out. Oops. One particular prisoner, James, is doing time for manslaughter."

"Wow," Colleen frowned.

"He has a wife and seven children. They live on a farm. I went over to visit them today, to see how they're getting along. Frances, James' wife, gave me the steaks."

"That was precious of her," Katherine said.

"Plus, I had an excuse to go see the kids. They are adorable. The eldest is fourteen and the youngest is five."

A seagull swooped overhead and landed next to Mum. Mum screamed.

Kate said, "He won't hurt you. He's just begging for food."

"Then I should give him some," Mum said, throwing out a piece of steak.

Kate suggested, "I wouldn't do that if I were you."

It was too late. A flock of seagulls descended and circled Mum.

"Get out of here!" Mum yelled, flapping her arms.

Katherine and Colleen burst out laughing.

"Serves you right," Katherine said.

*　　　*　　　*

At ten o'clock, the foursome walked back to their cabins. Kate headed for hers; Katherine and Colleen followed behind her with the dishes and utensils. Kate carried the cooler.

Colleen asked, "What about the beach blankets?"

"My uncle will pick them up."

Mum walked back to Cabin Three.

Katherine was the first to thank Kate.

Colleen invited Kate over for a night cap. "Join us for a drink on the screened-in porch. It's the last night we'll be able to do this. Our significant others arrive tomorrow."

"Sure, but let me bring the wine. I got it as a gift from the warden. It's a nice cabernet."

"You read my mind. My favorite wine is cabernet. Thanks," Katherine said.

Kate smiled. "Give me a minute, and I'll be there."

Katherine and Colleen walked back to their cabin. Mum shut the refrigerator door and sat down at the table. Her tumbler was filled to the top.

Colleen didn't notice, and walked to the bathroom.

Katherine knew mum had been helping herself to the boxed wine. She walked over to the refrigerator and opened the door. Inside were two more boxes of the wine. They hadn't been there earlier. She started to ask Mum about it, but she knew it would only cause an argument between mother and daughter, so she didn't. She thought, *Mum must have paid the limo service driver to go to a liquor store, as well.* She wondered when Mum had gone off the wagon, and hoped she'd seek help again once she was back in Manhattan.

Katherine went to her bedroom to check on the cats. Scout and Abra were lying on her bunk, spooned together. Scout was snoring; Abra had her lip pulled back with one fang showing.

Katherine said to the cats in a soft voice, "I guess you had too much excitement today. Sleep, my darlings. You're staying in this room tonight whether Colleen likes it or not." Then she remembered the door being open that morning when she had specifically closed it to keep the cats out the night before. She walked into the kitchen to ask Mum.

"Did you open our bedroom door this morning?"

Mum looked up from her tumbler, "No, I didn't, but—"

"Who did? I know I didn't."

"That Houdini cat of yours opened it with her brown little paws." Mum laughed.

Colleen came in the room and heard some of the conversation. "It was strange our door was open. Mum, if you didn't open it, who did?"

"'Twas the ghost — the one we heard last night. She did it. . . ." Mum couldn't finish, she was laughing too hard.

"Very funny," Colleen retorted, then said excitedly, "I completely forgot about this. Abra found a wallet on the beach. That's what she was digging for when I found her."

Katherine said, "Go get it, so we can look inside to see who it belongs to."

Colleen rushed to her bedroom, opened the first drawer of the dresser, and pulled out the wallet. She returned to the kitchen and handed it to Katherine.

Katherine took out the driver's license. "Arlo Komensky." She looked up at Colleen and Mum. "That's that guy who owns the cabins. The manager-maintenance man. I better walk over and return it to him."

132

"At this hour?" Mum asked in a worried tone.

"He might need it," Katherine said.

"Didn't Kate say no one was home. Why don't we both walk it over tomorrow?" Colleen suggested.

Mum offered, "When I checked in, I saw a drop box. It's right outside the door. Why don't the two of you return it in the morning. If no one is there, just drop it in the box."

Colleen nodded; Katherine didn't answer.

There was a knock at the door. Katherine moved to open it. "Come in," she greeted Kate.

Kate clutched a bottle of wine. She also held up a corkscrew. "In case you don't have one over here."

"Come sit in the living room," Katherine guided.

"Where are the cats?" Kate asked.

"In the bedroom, sleeping off their adventure."

Kate laughed. She sat down on the sofa; Mum joined her. Colleen took the chair closest to the fireplace. Katherine still held Arlo's wallet in her hand.

"Kate, one of my cats found the manager's wallet on the beach. I was going to return it."

"Misty's?"

"No, Arlo's."

"When I leave, I can walk it over. Maybe they'll be home by then," then Kate changed the subject. "Earlier, you said your significant others are coming tomorrow. Not that I'm nosy or anything, but where are they going to stay? Pretty cramped quarters in the cabin."

Katherine answered, "The guys are bringing their sleeping bags. They're going to camp out in the living room."

"Fun, just like summer camp. Who wants wine?" Kate asked, getting up and taking the bottle to the kitchen.

Mum said, "Not I."

Katherine said, "I'll take a glass."

"I'll pass. I'm going to drink water instead," Colleen said, holding up a bottle of spring water.

Kate returned and handed Katherine a goblet. She resumed her seat on the sofa and took a sip. "Tomorrow I have a second date with a man I reconnected with online. He's driving up, and taking me to lunch."

"That's nice," Katherine said.

"Several years ago, I helped him find an attorney. His wife back home had filed for divorce. They had a daughter and he wanted to make sure she was cared for.

He said his wife was into drugs, and once he got out of prison, he wanted to get custody of his daughter."

Colleen asked, "What was he doing time for?"

"Armed robbery, but I think he was at the wrong place at the wrong time."

"Armed robbery," Colleen said aghast.

"Actually, I don't think he had anything to do with it."

"I don't mean to sound sarcastic, but don't all criminals say that," Colleen noted.

Katherine asked, "So, how did you reconnect with him?"

"On Facebook. I was bored one night and keyed in some names of people I'd like to see if they were on Facebook, just curious about what happened to them. Sure enough, up popped his name. We started emailing each other, then we met last night."

Mum asked curiously, "He's no longer married?"

"No, they're divorced. In fact, she died. He has custody of his daughter."

"Is he bringing his daughter tomorrow?"

"No, it's just the two of us." Kate finished her glass, then got up. "Ladies, I must call it a day. I had so much fun."

"We did too," Mum said. "Thank you for everything," then, "I'm calling it a day, also." Mum headed to her bedroom.

Colleen said to Kate, "Have fun on your lunch date tomorrow."

"Yes, definitely."

Katherine walked Kate to the door. "Don't you want to take the rest of the bottle home?"

"No, you keep it. Oh, where's Arlo's wallet? I'll take it to him."

"Here," Katherine said, extracting the wallet from her pocket. She handed it to Kate.

Kate took the wallet, opened the door and walked out into the night.

Katherine watched her until she was out of sight, then went back inside. Suddenly, she felt uneasy. A strong sense that something wasn't right came over her.

Colleen came into the room. "What gives? You look like you've seen the ghost."

"Maybe we should make sure Kate gets home okay."

"Why?"

"Because all of the sudden, I have a bad feeling that something is going to happen to her."

"The manager's cabin is right next to Kate's. If the couple aren't home, she'll put it in the drop box, then go home."

Katherine closed the door and locked it. "I suppose you're right."

Colleen said, "I'm not really tired. I'll take that glass of wine now. I want to sit on the porch so I can listen to the waves. Maybe the sound will lull me to sleep."

"Sure. I'll pour you a glass. Be there in a minute."

Colleen moved to the porch, opened the connecting door from the living room, and said, "I still don't know what time the boys are showing up tomorrow. Daryl didn't text me."

"Jake was supposed to call me." Katherine's cell rang. She read his name on the screen of her phone. "Oh, there he is. It's about time!" She moved off to the kitchen to answer it. "Hi, Jake. Miss me?"

Jake answered, "I meant to call you earlier. Of course, I miss you and so do the cats. Iris has been yowling at the front door."

"Aw, poor Miss Siam. What time are Daryl and you arriving?"

"That's just it," Jake began. "We have a vehicle problem."

"What kind of vehicle problem?"

"My Jeep's in the shop."

"What's wrong with it?"

"Not sure. Maybe a bad alternator. It's being worked on tomorrow."

"Jake, precious, love of my life," Katherine began carefully because Jake loved his Jeep. "It may be time for you to part with the Jeep. Why don't you let me buy you another one?"

"Thanks, Katz, but I'll drive my Jeep until it falls apart."

"So how are you getting here?"

"Daryl said if it doesn't rain, we'll come in the Impala." Daryl drove a classic 1967 black Impala that he rarely drove unless he was taking it to an in-state car show.

"If it doesn't rain? What?"

"He doesn't like for the Impala to get wet."

"Oh, brother. Check the forecast."

"I did, and guess what, Sweet Pea. It's not going to rain. Expect to see us around noon."

"What time is Elsa coming to take care of the cats?"

"She'll be here at ten, so I can give her the key."

"Okay, can't wait for you to see how beautiful it is up here."

"Can't wait to see you," Jake said in a loving voice, then became serious. "I need to talk to you about something."

"You sound mysterious."

"Just a question I have for you."

"What?"

"I'd much rather ask you in person."

"Jake, spit it out?"

"It's nothing, oh, and before I hang up, you received a surprise gift."

"From whom?"

"I don't know."

"What is it?"

"A new Huffy bike, just like your old one except this one is a light blue."

"Dang that Stevie. I told him not too."

"Stevie bought it?" Jake asked with a jealous tone. "Why would he give you a new bike?"

Katherine heard the jealousy in Jake's voice and proceeded with caution. "The other day, when that psycho ran over my bike, Stevie felt responsible."

"Why?"

"Because Stevie knew the man. After the guy ran over my bike, Stevie said he was going to replace it, and I said no."

"Did he say who the guy was?"

"Not by name, but when I threatened to call Chief London, Stevie got upset and said the guy just got out of prison. He said my involving the police might jeopardize the guy's parole, so I dropped it."

"Well, Katz, I think you should ask Stevie if he gave you the bike. If Stevie didn't give it to you, maybe the psycho-parolee did."

"Whoever gave it to me, I'm not comfortable receiving gifts."

"Oh, you're not, are you?" Jake teased.

"I mean getting gifts from people I don't know."

"I'm not comfortable with a psycho-parolee coming up on our front porch," Jake said.

"My sentiments exactly."

"Listen, Sweet Pea. I have to hang up now. Love you. See you tomorrow."

"Love you too. Be careful." Katherine hung up.

*　　*　　*

Kate held Arlo's wallet and walked to the cabins' service road to go to the manager's office. The road was well-lit with security lights.

Something in the back of her mind warned her about danger. Her urban sense was on full alert. *Maybe I should turn back and return the wallet tomorrow,* she thought, then said out loud, "Chicken. Just get it over with. Do it now." She moved past her cabin and smiled at how security-conscious she was by leaving her cabin's outside lights on, so she wouldn't be afraid coming home from Katherine's. A little farther, she noticed the manager's Cherokee still wasn't in its parking space. The cabin lights were out, so she assumed the couple hadn't gotten home yet. *Easy-peasy,* she thought. *I'll drop the wallet in the box, then go home.*

141

Stepping up to the cabin's porch landing, she was surprised to see the manager's door partially open. She pushed it open, went inside and looked around. The bright moonlight illuminated the room.

Misty was sitting at the front desk. Kate startled. Her inner voice said *run*, but instead she approached the desk. She could see that Misty had a bruise under her eye and that her lip was bleeding.

"Hey, are you okay?" Kate asked. "Who did this to you?"

"What do you want?" Misty asked, irritated. "Can't you see we're closed?"

Kate was taken aback. She was surprised by Misty's unfriendly behavior. "I'm returning your husband's wallet."

"What are you doing with it?" Misty asked suspiciously.

Kate started to back out of the office. "I guess I caught you at a bad time. I'll just put it in the drop box."

"I asked you a question. How did you get it? Where was it?"

Kate didn't appreciate Misty's accusatory tone. "You know what, I'll give it to Arlo myself."

"Give it to me," Misty ordered.

Kate huffed out of the office and stomped back to her cabin. "What is her problem? Why is she being such a jerk?" she asked out loud. Arriving at her back door, she paused on the wood-planked landing and fumbled in her purse to find her key. A porch floorboard creaked behind her. She quickly turned to see who it was. She assumed it was Misty, but instead it was a man. He was wearing an old army-issue jacket and blue jeans. A black ski mask covered his head.

"Give me your money," he demanded.

Kate handed him her purse. The man dumped the contents on the porch, then picked up the wallet. He put it in his jacket's pocket, then grabbed Kate by her long hair and pulled her off the porch. She lost her balance and fell face-forward in the sand. When she tried to get up, the man kicked her several times in the ribs. The pain was so severe, she passed out.

*　　*　　*

An hour later, Misty continued sitting at her desk. She was sorry she'd been such a witch to Kate, who had always been nice to her. She buried her face in her hands. She sobbed until her black eye was throbbing, so she forced herself to stop. She dabbed her eyes with the corner of her sleeve.

Misty wanted to call the sheriff's department and report her abusive husband, but something inside advised her not to. Arlo was best friends with Sheriff Earle, who would naturally take Arlo's side. He'd done so in the past. Why should this time be any different? It wasn't the first time Arlo hit her. She'd given up calling 911. Besides, the last thing she wanted to do was call attention to herself, especially since Josh and she had cooked up a plan to get her out of her mess called a marriage.

On her desk, her cell phone buzzed. She picked it up. It was Josh.

"Hey, darling, are you at the truck stop, getting some rest?" she asked sweetly.

"We've got a little problem, but I've taken care of it."

"What are you talking about?"

"I took that Kate woman somewhere, so she'll be out of the way."

"What have you done?" Misty asked, horrified.

"I overheard her talking to you. She's hell-bent on returning Arlo's wallet. I didn't want her taking it to his cabin when I've got business to take care of."

Misty said, baffled, "What are you saying? Kate doesn't know Arlo moved out."

"I covered it, babe," Josh said.

"Did she see you?"

"No, I came up from behind."

"For the love of god, please tell me you didn't kill her?"

"No, dammit. I knocked her out . . . okay, listen, the battery on my phone is giving out. I'm in Arlo's cabin right now, waiting for him to get home."

Misty warned, "What? Arlo is there!"

"No, he's not. He must have fixed the pickup because it ain't parked out back either."

"Get out of there before he comes back! He's gone totally insane. He's armed. Don't go through with it."

"Wait! He just came in," Josh hung up.

"Oh, no . . . no . . . no, I have to stop this," she said, punching in Arlo's cell number. It rang several times, then went to voicemail.

Jumping out of her chair, she ran outside. She took the shortcut path in front of the cabins. She could see a man up ahead, taking the same path. She couldn't make out if it was Arlo or not, but she called out to him anyway. "Come back. Come back to me," she screamed.

The man glanced in her direction. "Any one there?"

Misty darted behind a boxwood shrub.

Two children ran out to greet him. "Daddy, where have you been?"

"I took a walk on the beach. What are you kids doing up so late?" he scolded. "Come on, I've got to put you to bed. Where's your mom?"

The trio walked into Cabin Five.

When Misty heard their door close, she proceeded to Cabin Six.

Chapter Ten

Late Friday Night

The Witching Hour

Katherine and Colleen relaxed on their Adirondack chairs and sipped their wine. They made light conversation, and were getting ready to call it a night, when Scout and Abra trotted in. Their tails were twice the normal size. The cats screeched in a shrill, high-pitched tone, "Mir-waugh . . . waugh . . . waugh!" They arched their backs and began their death dance, swaying back and forth, hopping up and down in front of the screened porch that overlooked the lake.

Katherine lunged out of her chair. "What's wrong?"

The Siamese stopped and stood tall, their ears swiveled in the direction of the beach.

Katherine and Colleen heard the pounding of someone running in front of the cabin. "Come back. Come back to me," a woman's voice screamed.

Scout cried a long, menacing growl.

Colleen launched out of her chair. "That wasn't a spirit."

Katherine picked up Abra and held her close. Talking in a soft voice, she said to the cat, "Everything is okay. I'm going to take you to the bedroom," then to Colleen, "Can you get Scout?"

Colleen said, "Sure." She walked over to pick up Scout, but the Siamese was frantically pawing at the torn screen.

Scout had been working on making the opening bigger since Katherine and Colleen arrived at the cabin. Finally, she succeeded. She disappeared through the opening and jumped down to the sandy yard.

Colleen panicked, "Katz, Scout got out."

Katherine didn't hear Colleen. She put Abra in the bedroom and shut the door. Abra howled on the other side like she was being murdered.

Colleen ran down the hall. "Didn't you hear me? Scout got out."

"Again?" Katherine asked incredulously. She yanked Scout's leash off the kitchen counter and hurried to the back door. "She probably ran back down to the beach."

"I'm coming, too."

"Grab a flashlight."

Colleen found the light on a hook by the door and jogged after Katherine. They took the path that ran in front of the cabins. The full moon cast an eerie shadow on the path. Twenty feet away, Scout sat on her haunches, staring at them.

"I see her," Katherine said. "Scout, wait for us."

Scout turned her head, then dashed to the front of Cabin Six. She stopped momentarily to see if the humans were following, then rounded the corner.

"Scout, stop!" Katherine commanded, to no avail.

Katherine and Colleen sprinted, but the loose sand prevented them from building up speed.

Scout peered around the corner of the cabin. "Waugh," she cried urgently, which sounded like *hurry up*.

Katherine said, catching her breath, "She wants us to follow her."

"You think?" Colleen said, trying to make light of the situation.

When Katherine caught up with Scout, the Siamese was very agitated. Katherine tried to snap the clasp of the leash on Scout's collar, but the cat darted away.

"Come back here," Katherine pleaded.

Scout ran and stopped in front of Cabin Six's side door, which was standing wide-open. She swiveled her ears forward then backward, in an inquisitive motion.

"Do *not* go in there," Katherine warned.

Scout rushed in and disappeared in the darkness.

"Just great," Katherine muttered.

Catching up, Colleen said, "This is creeping me out. I'm not going in there."

"Is anyone home?" Katherine called from the door. She rang the doorbell. "Hello, is anyone home?"

No one answered.

Colleen said, "Find a light switch."

Katherine found one inside the door and turned it on. She screamed and stepped back.

"What's wrong?"

"Look!" Katherine pointed at the man sprawled face-down in front of the fireplace.

Colleen gasped, "Is he dead?"

Katherine moved to find out, then heard something loud drop in the back of the cabin. She glanced down the hall. She saw the silhouette of a cat in front of a closed bedroom door.

"Scout, come here, darling. Come to mommy."

"Na-waugh," Scout cried. She stood up on her hind legs and tried to turn the door knob with her front paws.

"Hiss," the Siamese snarled.

Katherine dove for the cat, snatched her around the middle, and attached the clasp of the leash to Scout's collar.

Scout shrieked.

Katherine thought she heard movement on the other side of the door. She held onto Scout and flew past Colleen. "Let's get out of here."

Colleen ran behind her. "What's the plan?"

"We need to call 911."

"Now? Are you crazy?"

"Not now. We'll call when we get back home. Whoever murdered that man may still be in the cabin. They might come after us."

Colleen stumbled, but caught herself before falling on the sandy path. The flashlight flew out of her hands and fell down the dune. She quickly got up, squinted back at Cabin Six, to see if anyone was following them, then saw something in the corner of her eye. She looked in the direction of the beach. A shimmering shape hovered over the sand. The apparition was a woman, dressed in a long dress that billowed out around her. She had long hair, which whipped around her face as if the wind was caressing it.

When Katherine realized Colleen wasn't right behind her, she stopped, turned and stared down the path. Colleen was glued to the edge of the dune. Katherine said urgently, "Come on. We have to get inside."

"Look," Colleen said, pointing.

Katherine jogged back to Colleen. Her eyes followed where Colleen was pointing. They grew big in shocked surprise. "It's the ghost," she stammered, then tugged Colleen's arm. "Snap out of it! Come on."

Scout caught a glimpse of the specter and growled.

Colleen, once an active member of a ghost-hunting group, wanted to investigate, but her gut instinct said to go back to the cabin. She dashed past Katherine. "Go . . . go . . . go!"

Katherine chased after her with her nose buried in Scout's fur. "It's okay. We're almost there," she said, trying to calm the Siamese down.

Katherine and Colleen cut through the space between Cabin Four and Cabin Three.

Scout began to struggle. Katherine held her tighter. "Quit fighting me. We have to get inside."

"Waugh," Scout protested.

Colleen was the first to run through the back door, then Katherine, holding Scout.

Katherine quickly realized that in her haste to catch Scout, she'd forgotten to lock the cabin's door. She hurriedly locked it.

Colleen noticed it and said, "The killer could be in here."

"Shhh," Katherine shushed her. "I'm putting Scout in with Abra, and getting my Glock. You stay here. If anything happens, run to the manager's office."

"Be careful."

Katherine continued to hold Scout as she moved quietly to the bedroom. Abra began wailing on the other side of the door.

Great, Katherine thought. *Gee, thanks, Abra. Just announce to the killer that we're home.*

Katherine partially opened the door and stuck her foot in to prevent Abra from running out. She then set Scout down on the floor. Abra ran over to Scout and began washing her ears.

Katherine hurried inside, grabbed her gun from the chest of drawers, then darted back into the hallway. She quickly checked the bathroom, then sprinted to check on Mum. She opened the bedroom door and sighed with relief. Mum was in a deep sleep, and snoring. She quietly closed the door.

Katherine walked down the hall, and made sure the killer wasn't in the living room or on the screened-in porch. She then joined Colleen in the kitchen. Colleen had collapsed on a kitchen chair.

"There's no killer in the cabin, and Mum is sleeping."

"That's a relief. I'm so scared. I can hardly breathe."

"Me, too," she agreed, yanking her cell off the charger and punching in 911.

The dispatch operator answered, "911. What's your emergency?"

"My name is Katherine Cokenberger. I'm calling from the Seagull Cabins. My friend and I were taking a walk with our — I mean — my cat, and my cat got away and ran into Cabin Six."

"Ma'am, state your emergency?" the dispatcher asked firmly.

"The door to Cabin Six was open and my cat ran in. Inside, we found a man lying dead on the floor," Katherine explained in a terrified voice.

"Was it someone you know?"

"No, I've never seen this man before in my life." Katherine continued with more details, such as the address of the Seagull Cabins, and how she felt the murderer was still in the cabin in the back bedroom.

The operator asked, "Are you there now?"

"No, I'm in Cabin Three. I'm calling from Cabin Three," she repeated.

"Stay there, lock your doors, and wait for the sheriff to stop by and talk to you."

"Okay, will do." Katherine hung up.

Colleen asked, "What are we supposed to do?"

"Stay put until the sheriff gets here."

*   *   *

Back in Cabin Six, Misty sobbed in Josh's arms. "I told you not to go through with it." She shook uncontrollably.

"No, you didn't," he protested.

"I told you on the phone."

"You didn't," he continued. "Don't cry," he consoled. "I hate it when you cry."

Misty wiped away her tears with the back of her hand, careful not to touch her bruised eye. "What are we going to do? They're probably calling the sheriff right now."

"Who were those women? Did they see you come in here?"

"I don't think they saw me, but the family next door may have recognized me, especially the dad."

"What are you blathering about? What family next door?"

"The family of four that are staying for two weeks."

"So?"

"I was on the path in front of the cabins. I thought I saw Arlo walking ahead, so I called out to him. When the man turned and glanced back at me, I realized it was the dad of the family that checked in."

"Then what did you do?"

"I didn't have to do anything because his kids ran out to greet him, and they all went inside their cabin."

"Where were you when you called out to him?"

"Close to Cabin Three."

156

"I'm bankin' he didn't see you. Now back to my original question. Who were those women?"

"I think it was the gals who rented Cabin Three."

"What do you mean, you think it is? Didn't you check them in?"

Misty shook her head. "When I checked in the mother, she said the other two in her party would be arriving shortly. The online reservation was made by a woman named Katherine. I spoke to her yesterday. She said her water heater was broken. I never heard back from her, so I think Arlo took care of it."

"Do these gals have a dog? What was that thing snarling and scratching at the door?"

"It sounded like a cat."

"How would you know that?"

"Dogs don't hiss. When Katherine booked online she stated she had two cats. I think one of the cats got outside, and the women were trying to catch it. That dumb cat led them right here."

"That wouldn't have happened if you'd shut the damn door when you came in," Josh criticized.

"How was I supposed to do that when you yanked me back to the bedroom?" She started crying again, "I was too upset when I saw Arlo lying dead on the floor."

"Calm down," Josh demanded. "You have to keep a level head about this."

"How can I do that when you murdered my husband?" she cried.

Josh pushed her away, and gave an angry look. "If you back out of this now, so help me, you'll wish you'd never met me."

"Are you threatening me?"

"I'm sorry. I didn't mean what I said," Josh said, calming down. "I injected your old man with a hefty dose of that drug you told me to use. It stopped his heart pronto. The coroner will think Arlo kicked the bucket from natural causes."

"I'm getting sick," Misty said, sitting down on the bed.

"Get up. We have to get out of here." Josh grabbed Misty by the arm and led her to the cabin door. Misty looked at her prone husband, and covered her mouth to not scream, then she composed herself. "Are you sure you were careful not to touch anything?" She'd watched enough crime shows to know how incriminating evidence is left at a crime scene.

"Touch anything," he repeated. "My fingerprints are everywhere. I work here, remember? My prints are all over the place and so are yours."

"Are your prints on Arlo?"

"Do you think I'm stupid? I wore gloves."

Misty looked at her husband's body. "It doesn't look like there was a struggle. Why is that?"

"He came in the cabin and went to the fireplace. He was turning on the switch to the gas log, when I came up behind him. I stuck the needle in his neck. The drug was so fast, he didn't have time to react. He just fell on the floor."

"Is the syringe still stuck in his neck?" Misty panicked.

Josh patted his jacket pocket. "I'll get rid of it when I go check on that woman."

Misty looked at Josh like he'd lost his mind. "Then what? Kill her. Where is she?"

"At that abandoned trailer up the road from here."

"You left here there? With the crazy homeless man who lives there?" Misty asked, shocked.

"There wasn't anybody there."

"Did Kate recognize you?"

"I told you already. I came up from behind and put her in a chokehold. I guess I don't know my own strength. She wasn't moving, so I let go, then she started to fight. I smacked her around a little, then she fell and hit her head," he said, lying about what really happened. He left out the part about kicking Kate in her ribs.

"Okay, enough. I don't want to hear any more. Kate will come to and make her way back here," Misty said, then added, "That is, if she's still alive."

Josh glared at her. "I didn't kill her."

"Let's go," Misty said nervously. "You go to your cabin. Get rid of the syringe tomorrow. Keep a low profile. Got it?"

They both heard sirens wailing in the distance.

Josh took her arm and directed her out the door.

"Josh, I'll be the number one suspect, so do not, absolutely do not, try and call me or come and see me. In a week, I'll meet you at the place we talked about."

"I've changed my mind. That's a ridiculous plan. I work for you. The sheriff will suspect me if I don't show up for work on Monday."

"All right, have it your way," Misty said, throwing her hands up in exasperation.

"Get moving," Josh said. "You go back to your cabin. When the sheriff knocks on your door, take forever to get there. Tell him you've been asleep. When he tells you Arlo is dead, start crying your eyes out. Got it?"

"Okay." Misty started for the path in front of the cabins.

"Don't go that way," Josh warned. "Climb down the dune and take the beach route. Come up on the lake access road. You don't want anyone at the cabins bumping into you."

"You're nuts. I'm not going down there at night. The damn beach is haunted. I'll take my chances," she said, walking to the path in front of the cabins.

Chapter Eleven

Waiting for the Sheriff

Colleen paced the floor in the kitchen. "What's taking the sheriff so long? You don't think he'll make us go back and identify the body?"

"Why would he do that? We don't know who the victim is."

"I wish I had Kate's number."

"Why?"

"So, I can text her about the murder. Maybe we should walk over and let her know. Maybe we should call the manager?"

"Let's do what the sheriff wants us to do. Sit tight until he gets here to talk to us." Katherine peeked out the kitchen window at Kate's cabin. "Her outside lights are on, but the rest are off. She probably turned in for the night."

"I'd like to be in my bed too," Colleen lamented. "That poor man. I wonder who he is — I mean — was?"

"I hope the sheriff can tell us."

"Are you going to tell him about Scout leading us to the crime scene?"

"Ah, no," Katherine said adamantly.

"What are you going to say?"

"The bare facts. We heard a woman run by our cabin. She was screaming bloody murder. She scared my cat who tore a hole in the screen and got out. I'm going to say exactly what I told the dispatcher."

"You know Scout deliberately led us there. She was waiting for us to catch up."

"I'm leaving out that part."

The loud sound of sirens pierced the night. Colleen and Katherine hurried to the back door and peered out the curtain. Driving down the service road, the sheriff's SUV was first, then followed by two deputies in separate vehicles. An ambulance arrived last. They all parked behind Cabin Six.

Katherine and Colleen walked back into the kitchen, sat down at the table, and waited for the sheriff to come. They didn't wait long. A heavy knock sounded on the door.

"That was fast," Katherine said, surprised. She got up and answered the door.

The sheriff, with a large belly and a booming voice to match, stormed in. He was as friendly as a rattlesnake. "Which one of you called this in?" he demanded.

Katherine replied softly, "I did, Sir."

"I should charge you with false reporting. What kind of joke is this?"

"I'm not joking."

"There isn't a body in Cabin Six. There isn't a murderer in the back room."

"But . . . but. . . my friend and I saw a man lying dead on the floor."

"I want to see some IDs . . . now," he said brusquely.

Katherine reached for her bag, which was on the table. Colleen grabbed hers from the half wall in the kitchenette. Katherine showed her license first.

The sheriff studied the driver's license. "Katherine Cokenberger. Erie, Indiana. Where's Erie?"

"West Central Indiana, close to the Illinois border."

He returned Katherine's license, then studied Colleen's. "Colleen Murphy. Lafayette, Indiana. I know where Lafayette is. Is Erie close-by?"

"Less than an hour drive," Colleen said nervously.

The sheriff caught the nervous inflection in Colleen's voice and became even more suspicious than he was. He handed Colleen's license back. "Here's a question. Have you two been drinking?" the sheriff accused, now studying Colleen. "Are you intoxicated or impaired in any way?"

"No, we're not drunk," Colleen reassured.

"Do you think it's a joke getting us out here for nothing? We work hard during the day and deserve our rest."

Katherine didn't know what to say, then asked, "Are you sure you went to the right cabin?"

The sheriff gave her a cold look. "We went to the cabin with a big six on the back door. No body. No blood-splatter. No dead person."

Colleen said, "I saw him, too." She repeated Katherine's account verbatim, but left out the part about Scout leading them to the scene.

Katherine said, "I know what I saw."

The sheriff continued in his loud voice, "And this is what I saw — an empty cabin."

Colleen asked, "Did you search the back bedrooms? We heard a loud noise come from back there."

The sheriff eyed Colleen curiously, then said, "Haven't you been paying attention? I just said there was no murderer back there. The only thing we found in the

cabin was a very angry raccoon who hissed at my deputy."
The sheriff turned to the officer standing behind him.
"Isn't that right, Howard?"

"Yep, hissed at me, then tore out of the cabin like a
racehorse. I didn't know raccoons could run so fast."

The sheriff laughed a loud belly laugh. "Well, Ms.
Cokenberger, you've been the butt of a practical joke.
Some of the local hooligans, probably teenagers, really had
you going. One of them deliberately ran by your cabin,
then led you to a fake crime scene. You two gullible
women fell for it — hook, line and sinker."

"Sheriff, I beg to differ. Could you please call
Misty, the manager, and find out who rented Cabin Six?"

"What's that going to tell us?"

"Misty told my friend's mom that the cabins were
fully booked this week. I'm just interested in what she has
to say about hooligans renting one of her cabins."

The sheriff shot Katherine a dirty look. He dug out
his cell and punched in a number. He spoke into the phone,
"Sorry, Misty, about getting you up. There's been a little
mix-up here with two of your guests staying in Cabin
Three. They think they found a dead body in Cabin Six.
Yeah, dead body," he repeated. "Oh, oh. Big argument,

huh? Okay, case closed. Thanks, darlin'. Tell Arlo when he wakes up to slow down on his drinkin'." The sheriff disconnected the call.

"Who rented the cabin?" Katherine asked adamantly.

"Your friend's mom was wrong about the cabins being fully booked this week. Cabin Six is vacant. The man you thought was dead was the owner, Arlo. Misty said they had a big fight. He moved into Cabin Six. He got drunk, then came crawling back home to her. She said he was sleeping it off, in their bed. She apologized for disturbing you."

Katherine started to protest, but bit her lip to keep quiet.

The sheriff returned to his stern voice, "Next time you call my department this late at night, you better be sure of what you're reporting, because the next time I *will* charge you. Good night." He tipped his tasseled hat and left.

Katherine followed the sheriff, shut the door and locked it.

"Katz, this is ridiculous."

"I totally agree."

"I'm not impressed with the sheriff's police work nor his patronizing tone. He's quick to jump to conclusions. First, the lame hooligan theory, and then the drunk owner story."

"Something is off. In Cabin Six, did you see any signs of drinking?"

"Nope, not one liquor bottle. In fact, the place looked like it had been cleaned and was ready for the next guest."

"I think the murderer moved the body before the sheriff got there. I'd say right after we left."

"But Misty said her husband was at home with her."

Katherine shrugged her shoulders. "We don't know what her husband looks like. Maybe it was somebody else lying dead on the floor."

"The scary part is, whoever did this could have murdered us," Colleen said.

"I know. We got lucky. I'm going to investigate this tomorrow, but I'm too tired to do so tonight."

"Who am I? Chopped liver? I'm investigating, too. But not now. I'm ready to collapse on the floor. Let's go to bed."

Mum padded into the kitchen wearing her fuzzy house slippers. "What's going on?" she asked sleepily. "I heard the sirens and thought I was back in New York. Who was that man yelling?"

Katherine explained, "Oh, it's nothing. Scout got out again and there was drama catching her."

Mum repeated, "Who was that man yelling his head off?"

"The sheriff. He was annoyed at us for calling 911," Colleen explained.

Mum asked, "Why would you call the sheriff about Scout getting out?"

Katherine thought fast. She didn't want to upset Mum or stay up any later explaining in minute detail what had transpired. "Oh, you know, how hysterical I get when one of my cats get out."

"I wouldn't say hysterical but you do get very upset. Okay, love," Mum said, heading back to her bedroom.

After mum closed her door, Colleen said, "We can tell her tomorrow."

"I vote we sleep in."

"Deal!"

Chapter Twelve

Early Saturday Morning

Pink Mansion

Daryl, Jake's blond-haired, green-eyed cousin, drove his classic car in front of the pink mansion and parked.

Jake was standing on the front porch waiting for him. He grabbed his overnight bag and walked to the car.

The Impala's door made a creaking sound when Daryl got out. "Howdy, Cousin. Throw your bag on the back seat."

Jake opened the door to find a large flower arrangement covering most of the seat. "Somebody die?" Jake asked facetiously.

Daryl laughed. "I think there's room on the floorboard."

Jake came around and wedged his bag behind Daryl's seat.

"Colleen likes flowers," Daryl explained. "Plus, her mother will be there. It's for the both of them."

Jake walked back to the other side of the car and climbed in the passenger seat. "Always good to butter up your future mother-in-law."

"Exactly." Daryl put the Impala in gear and pulled out. "I think I'll take 41 to Kentland, then head over to the interstate. That beats a lot of stop-and-goes."

"Ah, our gals took the stop-and-go route. Maybe we should go that way."

"Hey, Cuz, driver picks the route. Stop-and-go route," Daryl snickered. "That's why it took them almost three hours to get there."

Daryl floored the accelerator and raced out of Erie.

"Whoa, slow down," Jake complained.

"Hey, I'm a cop. I know how to drive."

"No arguments there, but slow down so I can catch my breath."

Daryl laughed, then slowed down to the speed limit. "Is that better, Granny Two-Shoes?"

"I want to get there in one piece," Jake mumbled.

"I heard that," Daryl laughed again. "We should get to the cabin by noon. I figured the girls will be hungry, so I packed a cooler full of food."

"You packed a cooler," Jake laughed. "Let me guess. We'll have bologna sandwiches and Twinkies for dessert."

"Very funny. The cooler was my mom's idea."

"I hope Aunt June packed it."

"Of course."

"Hope she made her famous deviled eggs."

"Just for you."

"Cool, I'll have to give her a big hug next time I see her."

"Mom also made chicken and tuna salads, pickled beets, and baked oatmeal-raisin cookies."

"Pull over, so we can bust out the cookies."

"Sorry, Cuz. You'll have to wait for it. I figure we can have a picnic on the beach. I checked the weather app. Supposed to be in the 60s."

"Where's the cooler?" Jake asked, still thinking about the cookies.

"In the trunk. It weighs too much to set it on the back seat."

"Weighs too much? Can't be that heavy."

"I don't want any divots or tears. My fifty-one-year-old baby has its original upholstery."

"I learn something every day."

Daryl became serious. "There's something you need to be aware of."

Jake turned in his seat and studied Daryl's face. "What gives? You're not having second thoughts about getting married, are you?"

"No way. I'm not sure why you'd even ask that question. I fell for Colleen the first moment I saw her. I knew right then and there that I was going to marry her."

"Pretty sure of yourself, huh, buddy," Jake teased. "When was that?"

"Remember that fish fry we went to? You were dating Katz. Colleen was in town. Somehow, I forget how, I ended up being her date. It was during the Covered Bridge festival."

"In 2014. Wow, I can't believe that's been four years ago. A lot has happened since then. What was it about the fish fry that sparked a fire?"

"When I pulled the Impala in front of your house, well, Katz's house then, Colleen was all excited and knew it was a '67."

"Oh, I'd forgotten that. She used to go to classic car shows with her brothers. So, you're marrying Colleen because she loves your car?" Jake burst out laughing.

"Sort of. Plus, she's smart, funny, and doesn't take any crap off of me. I can't believe she'd find me even remotely attractive."

"Why would you say that? You're a Cokenberger. Cokenberger men aren't ugly."

"New York City gal falling for a county, small-town deputy."

"I'm privy to some inside information, but you must never tell Katz I told you."

"I can keep a secret."

"Colleen has not been lucky in the men department. Before you, the last guy she dated dumped her to go live in Italy."

"She never told me about it."

"Probably because the relationship didn't last very long."

"Yeah, I'm glad it didn't," Daryl smirked.

"Okay, but what is it you want to tell me? We got off the subject."

"Yesterday, Dad was in town and had lunch with your dad at the diner. Did he mention anything to you?"

"No, I haven't talked to my dad since last weekend. Why?"

"Sit tight. You're not going to like this."

"Dammit, Daryl, tell me," Jake said, aggravated.

"There's a terrible rumor going around town that Katz is having an affair."

Jake said angrily, "That's insane. Who's saying something ridiculous like that?"

"The gossips down at the Erie diner."

"Why are they saying this? And, who is she supposedly having an affair with?"

"Stevie Sanders."

Jake's face reddened with anger, but he forced a laugh. "Stevie Sanders? Him again?"

"What?" Daryl asked.

"Katz considers Stevie her friend. He's helped her out several times when her life was in danger."

"Yes, but that was several years ago. If that was the case, the gossips would have made up something then."

"No, they were too busy starting a witch hunt that nearly got Lizzie Howe lynched."

175

"Dad said someone at the diner said he saw Stevie with Katz at this BBQ joint in Rensselaer."

"Rensselaer. That's miles from Erie. When?"

"Thursday night."

"Thursday night," Jake repeated, skeptical. "Katz was with Colleen and her mother in Seagull."

"I know! We *know*, but whoever is spreading this lie doesn't know that."

"I'm going to find out who started it, and their head is going to roll."

"Just for the record, the Cokenberger brothers are all over it."

"What?"

"My dad, your dad, and Uncle Cokey. They have a short list of suspects, one of them is that liar, Jimbo Bell."

"Jimbo? He's the one who started it?"

"You seem surprised."

"I've known Jimbo for years. I wonder why he wouldn't come to me in the first place, before he blabbed it at the diner?"

"Because Jimbo didn't want you to ring his bell."

"Into next week, you mean. When I get back, I'm going to pay Jimbo a little visit."

"Maybe I should go, too," Daryl suggested.

"Why?"

"For Jimbo's protection," Daryl commented.

"Thanks, Cousin. Appreciate it, but I don't need you with Marine and law enforcement training to handle this one. I just want to talk to him." Jake became very quiet and didn't talk for a few minutes, then said, "I wish Stevie hadn't moved next to us."

"Why?"

"Because I know he's had a thing for my wife since day one."

"Have you talked to him about it?"

"Not yet. But, I'm going to let him know about this rumor."

"That won't go over well. I've seen the violent side of Stevie Sanders and it's not pretty."

"Yesterday, he bought her a bike and put it on the front porch. That sends off the wrong signal." Jake proceeded to tell Daryl about the wrecked bike incident. "Katz said someone Stevie knew in the past stopped by and the two of them got into an argument."

"Word travels fast. The guy who ran over Katz's bike was a cellmate of Stevie's — when Stevie was doing time in Michigan City. His name is Josh Williams. Apparently, they're not friends."

"You're a deputy in the next county. How did you find this out?"

"Sheriff Johnson told me. Ever since I shot and killed Stevie's father—"

Jake interrupted, "In the line of duty."

"Yes, this is true. The sheriff has kept me updated on the comings and goings of Stevie's family, including his brother, Dave."

"Does he think someone from the Sanders bunch will come after you?"

"Don't know. One can never predict these things. We're still not one-hundred-percent sure that the Sanders clan has gone clean."

"I can tell you this, as much as Stevie gets on my nerves, he's not a criminal. He's very good with his daughter."

"Exactly."

Chapter Thirteen

While Katherine and Colleen slept in, Mum finished packing. She'd called the airline and changed her ticket. Then, she'd called the limo service to take her back to the airport in Gary. Scout and Abra were helping her pack by jumping in-and-out of her open suitcase.

"You two have a ticket to be terrible. Go wake the girls up, so I can tell them good-bye."

Scout and Abra didn't have to be asked twice. They scampered out of the room and trotted into Katherine's and Colleen's bedroom. Abra used the windowsill to launch to the top bunk, while Scout jumped on Katz.

Katherine was lying on her back. Scout stood on top of her and pawed her face. "Go away. I'm trying to sleep," she complained.

Colleen woke up, "Get out of here," she yelled. Abra jumped back to the windowsill and pouted. Colleen sat up in bed and apologized to the Siamese, "Aww, I'm sorry. I didn't mean to hurt your feelings," then she muttered, "I'm completely daft for saying 'I'm sorry' to a cat."

Mum walked in. "Did my partners-in-crime help get you two up?"

"Good morning, Mum."

"Morning," Katherine said, sitting up. "Look at you — already up and dressed already."

Colleen said sleepily, "You don't have to make an impression for Daryl."

"Girls, I've changed my flight plans. I'm leaving this morning."

Colleen dangled her legs over the side of the bunk bed. "What? Why?"

"Oh, I don't want to be here when the lads arrive. I'd be like a fifth wheel, getting in everyone's way."

"Nonsense," Katherine protested.

"Mum, this was part of the girls' retreat plan. You've known since day one that Daryl and Jake were joining us today."

"I've done enough damage since I've been here. You can't talk me out of it. My limo will be here any minute."

Katherine said, "Limo service? I can drive you to the airport."

"Thank you, dear, but I can fend for myself."

Outside the cabin, the limo driver honked the horn.

"He's here. Can one of you help me carry my bag to the door?"

Colleen climbed down the bunk bed ladder. She threw on her robe and slipped into her slippers. "I'll help."

Katherine threw on her robe. "Me, too."

"Waugh," Scout said.

Mum laughed and said to Scout, "Thank you for your kind offer, but you've already helped me pack my suitcase."

"Raw," Abra cried. Mum walked over and petted Abra on the head. "I'll miss you." Scout trotted over for pets, too.

A knock sounded on the cabin's back door. Mum hurried out of the room. "I better get a move on or he'll leave me."

"How do you know it's not a female driver?" Colleen asked, walking into Mum's room and tugging the suitcase off the bed.

Mum rushed to the door and opened it a few inches. "One minute, please," she said to the driver. "Oh, no, don't come in. We have cats here and I don't want to let them out."

Katherine thought, *if only she'd thought of that when she told the fireman to check on the cats, then he opened a window without a screen.* Katherine walked over and hugged Mum. "I guess I won't see you until the wedding."

"Yes, love."

Colleen said, "I get a hug, too."

Mum embraced her daughter. "I love you. Tell Daryl I said hello."

A tear formed in Colleen's eye. "I love you, too. Text me when you get to the airport."

"I most certainly will do that."

Colleen opened the door and walked outside. She handed the limo service driver, a woman, her mother's bag. She gave an *I told you so* wink to Katherine, who held Mum's arm and was guiding her to the car.

Mum got in and smiled. "Katz, I'm really truly sorry about your cats getting out. I wasn't thinking."

"Water under the bridge," Katherine said, then smiled. "Be careful getting home."

"I will."

The driver closed the trunk, then Mum's door. She climbed in behind the steering wheel and drove down the service road.

Colleen and Katherine stood outside the cabin and watched Mum leave. They waved, then Katherine asked, worried, "Is she going to be okay?"

Colleen shook her head. "In a minute, I'm texting Jacky to see if he'll take Mum back to that alcohol addiction center. I don't trust her to do it herself."

"Good idea. Let's head back in. My feet are freezing."

Colleen looked over at Katherine's feet. "Where's your slippers?"

Katherine snickered. "I'm waiting for Prince Charming to bring them."

Colleen chuckled, "That's my line. You already have your Prince Charming," then asked, "I wonder what time it is?"

"Around ten."

Colleen became very animated. She said frantically, "I have to curl my hair." She rushed back to the cabin.

Katherine called after her, "If you'd cut your hair short like mine, you wouldn't have to bother."

*   *   *

Kate woke up in a small, dark room. She was lying on her side. She tried to sit up, but the pain was too much. Her ribs felt like they'd been hit by a sledge hammer.

The room had an overpowering, foul smell to it. The torn vinyl floor reeked of stale beer and rotten food. A sliver of light shone through the tattered curtain to show rubbish piled along the room's perimeter: mostly crumpled newspapers, cardboard boxes and empty food cans.

She couldn't remember ever feeling so awful. Her head throbbed and her stomach hurt. She was disoriented, then remembered she had been assaulted the night before by someone she couldn't even identify.

She remembered trying to return Arlo's wallet, but Misty was in a bad mood, so she went home. She couldn't find her keys and was rummaging around her purse, when a man came up behind her and demanded money. She gave him her purse, but he wasn't satisfied with that. He pushed her off the porch, then started kicking her. The pain was so severe, she passed out.

Where am I, she wondered. She carefully got up and felt her way to the window. With her left arm, she moved the curtain to the side. Sunlight poured in. She could see the dust raining down from the filthy curtain. She coughed, which caused a stabbing pain on her right side.

Looking out the dirty window, she could see a wooded area in the back. A rusted, broken-down pickup was jacked up on cinder blocks; its tires were missing. There was a sandy lane that didn't look like it had been used very much, except for the vehicle that had brought her here. She searched for that vehicle and was relieved she didn't see it. *But that doesn't mean he's not close by. Take it in baby steps*, she thought.

She limped to the closed door, turned the handle, and opened the door. She stepped on something sharp and realized she was walking without shoes. She said in angry voice, "The jerk took my shoes!"

Examining her foot and not seeing any blood, she walked slowly down a narrow hall, which led to a small living room/kitchenette combo. The front door was standing open. She glanced around the room and discovered she was in some kind of old mobile home.

A pile of garbage and old clothes were next to the door. She sorted through the pile and found an old pair of men's sneakers. Sitting down on a wood chair, she grimaced as she put the soiled shoes on. They were several sizes too big, but she put them on anyway. The hard part was tying the laces. Every time she leaned down to tie the shoes, an excruciating pain stabbed her right side. Finally, she tied them. She did a final search of the room but didn't find her purse or shoes. She stepped out of the trailer and struggled down two steps.

She said to herself, talking out loud, "There has to be a road nearby. You have to force yourself to find it. It hurts like hell, but you have to keep walking. Don't stop. You can do this, Kate. You can do this."

She studied the tire indentations on the lane and followed them away from the trailer. She caught a distant memory of something she'd learned in Girl Scouts. She thought, *the Sun rises in the east and sets in the west. If I'm walking south in the morning, the sun is on my left.* "I think that's what I learned. If I'm walking north I'll end up in the Lake. If I'm walking south I'll find some kind of road." Then she worried, *What if I find a road and some lunatic picks me up? That would be my luck.* Suddenly she wished she hadn't recently binged on true crime books. Every scary scenario popped up in her mind — every one of them leading to her being murdered at the end of the story.

"Forget it! Keep walking! Shut up, inner voice. My side is killing me," she said aloud.

Chapter Fourteen

Katherine and Colleen had returned to their Adirondack chairs on the screened-in front porch. Scout and Abra were busy stalking a large ant, which managed to dodge their pounces. Jake had called earlier and said they'd be arriving soon. He said Daryl was gassing up the Impala. He'd made a joke about the gas station in Seagull named Gas and Gull. Katherine laughed and said the town was obsessed with seagulls.

After a few minutes, Colleen said, "I hope they're getting here soon, because I'm starving to death."

"Me, too. Jake said they're bringing us lunch."

The Siamese stopped what they were doing and looked inside the cabin. They flicked their ears and muttered something in Siamese.

A loud knock sounded on the cabin's back door.

Katherine got out of her chair. "Surely that can't be them. Jake just called."

"Want me to get it," Colleen said, not moving from her chair.

"I'll get it, carrot top," Katherine snickered. She walked to the door and opened it. Stevie Sanders stood outside.

Stevie took a step backwards. "Katz," he said, surprised. "What are you doing here?"

"I can ask the same. What are you doing here?"

Stevie winked and flashed a handsome smile. "You go first."

"Colleen and I are here. We rented a cabin."

"Yes, the girls' retreat. I had no idea it was in Seagull. What a coincidence?"

"How?"

"I've got a date with a gal who lives next door to you."

"Who?" Katherine asked, stepping through the doorway and onto the rear small porch. Normally, Stevie didn't divulge personal information, but he'd just mentioned he had a date.

"Her name is Kate Allen. Have you met her?"

Katherine continued staring at Stevie like she was seeing things, then said, "Yes. We've met Kate. She's very nice. Last night, she grilled steaks for us."

"Her car is parked outside, but she's not answering the door. Any idea where she is?"

Katherine glanced over at Kate's rear parking area. She could see Stevie's truck parked behind Kate's Prius. "Not sure. We haven't seen her since last night. Maybe she took a walk on the beach."

Both Katherine and Stevie startled when they heard the loud engine roar of the Impala pulling in.

Daryl parked.

"What's he doing here?" Jake asked, fuming.

Daryl advised, "Only fools rush in."

"That's a bunch of crap," Jake answered. He got out of the car and walked over to Katherine and Stevie. He wore an angry expression on his face. "Hey, Stevie, what are you doing here?" he asked with an unfriendly tone.

Stevie's grin quickly changed to a frown.

Daryl joined Jake on the sidewalk.

Katherine said, "Stevie has a date with the woman who lives next door. She wasn't home, so he came over to ask if I knew where she was."

Jake continued his angry look at Stevie.

Stevie put his hands up. "I've got no quarrel here. I'm spending the day with the gal next door, but she's not home. I'll head on back to her place." Stevie started to walk away.

Katherine shot Jake a cold look that combined disapproval with surprise, then said to Stevie, "Wait a minute. If she doesn't return home soon, would you let me know?" Katherine suddenly became very worried.

"Yep," Stevie said, walking back to Kate's cabin, but stopped to get something out of his truck.

Daryl appraised the tension between husband and wife. He thought it wise to give them some space. "I'll get the cooler," he said. He headed back to the Impala.

Katherine snapped at Jake, "What was that about? You looked like you wanted to bite Stevie's head off." Her green eyes became mere slits.

Jake shuffled his feet and looked guilty. "Sorry, I didn't understand the situation. There's a back story to this. I'll tell you about it later. Can I come in now?"

"Sure," Katherine said, wearing a riled look. "I'll let Colleen know you guys are here."

"I'll grab my bag out of the car," Jake said, still in an annoyed mood.

"We're on the screened-in porch," she said, slamming the back door.

Stevie took the cue of Katherine going back inside to return to Jake. He held a piece of paper in his hand.

Jake stopped and glared at Stevie.

Stevie was angry. "If you've got something to say to me, say it, and stop pussy-footing around."

Jake's face reddened. "I do have something to say to you. I don't want you around my wife. I know you have a thing for her. Now half the town is saying you two are having an affair."

"I'd love to," Stevie said defiantly.

"What do you mean?"

"I mean that someday she'll get sick of you, never being around when she needs you — like when she's in trouble or something — because you never seem to be there for her when she is."

"That's none of your business," Jake retorted.

"Oh, yeah, not my business," Stevie repeated. "I've saved her from harm's way, hell, I won't mince words, from getting killed a number of times. And, where were you? If I had a woman like Katz, I'd never leave her alone and go wherever you go off to."

"That's right, Stevie. You never will have a woman like Katz."

Stevie turned and started to walk away. He said under his breath, "That's because one day she's gonna be mine." He threw the piece of paper on the ground and stormed off.

Daryl came over and picked it up.

Jake was furious. "I want to punch his lights out," he said.

"Calm down there, tiger," Daryl said, reading the document. "Wow, Cuz, he was telling the truth." He handed the sheet of paper to Jake. "He really is here to date a gal. Her name is Kate, and look at her picture."

"What about it?" Jake said, not looking.

"She's a dead ringer for Katz."

*   *   *

An hour later, Katherine and Jake sat on a plaid blanket on the beach, close to the path that led to it. Daryl and Colleen took a walk on the beach and were almost out of view. The couple walked hand-in-hand. Katherine was happy for them, but depressed by the news Jake had just told her.

"I'm sorry, Sweet Pea," he said. "Small-town, bored people make up things to entertain themselves and others."

"I could care less about the diner gossips. I know the people who mean the most to me would never believe it in a million years, which brings me to you. Did you believe it? Is that why you were so rude to Stevie?"

"I didn't believe it, but when I drove up and saw Stevie here, for one second, I didn't know what to think."

"There's no need to be jealous."

Jake said defensively, "I'm not jealous. Why would I be jealous of Stevie?"

"Okay, you're not jealous. I'm embarrassed I have to tell Stevie what the Erie yahoos are saying."

"I'll do it."

"Seriously, Jake? The way you treated him back there. He'll probably never speak to you again."

Stevie walked down the path. Jake was the first to greet him. "Hey, Stevie, want to join us? We've got cookies," he said in a feigned friendly tone.

Stevie stared at Jake and didn't answer. Instead he said to Katherine, "I'm heading back to Erie."

"Kate didn't return home?" she asked with rising concern.

Stevie shook his head. "I guess she didn't want to go out with me, but I'd wished she'd texted me. Two hours driving to be stood up is a little bit too much for my ego."

Jake blurted, "I'm sorry I was rude earlier."

Stevie hesitated, then answered, "No problem."

Katherine said in a concerned tone, "Stevie, late last night Kate left my cabin to walk to the front office."

"Why did she go there?" Jake asked.

"To return a wallet." Katherine proceeded to tell Stevie and Jake how Abra came upon the wallet and why Kate returned it. "In light of what happened at one of the cabins last night, I think we need to go to office and see if she returned it."

Stevie asked, "What happened in one of the cabins?"

Katherine explained. "After Kate left, Scout got out. Colleen and I caught her in Cabin Six. Inside we found a man lying on the floor. He looked dead, but when we heard a noise in another part of the cabin, we ran out. We hurried back to our cabin, and I called the sheriff. He investigated and said there wasn't a dead man in Cabin Six. He accused Colleen and me of false reporting."

Jake broke in, "Why didn't you tell me this when I got here?"

Katherine frowned at him, then turned to Stevie. "With Kate's car parked in back and her not answering the door, we need to check it out."

Katherine started to get up. Stevie extended his hand and helped her.

Jake said, "I'm coming, too."

Stevie's expression turned to worry. He didn't answer, but instead sprinted down the beach in the opposite direction.

"Where's he going?" Jake asked.

Katherine noticed the trio first. Daryl and Colleen were helping a woman walk. She had long black hair and was limping. "Kate," she shouted. "Jake, it's Kate. Something's happened to her."

Jake and Katherine ran as fast as they could on the sandy beach. Stevie had already caught up with the group.

Daryl spoke first, "I called an ambulance. They won't be here for twenty minutes."

Colleen added, "The 911 operator told us to head to the lake access road by the manager's cabin."

"That's quite a hike," Jake complained. "I can't believe the operator wants you to walk an injured person to a location because it's convenient for them."

"Stop walking," Stevie said, standing in front of Kate. "Kaitlyn, are you okay?" he asked in a gentle voice. "Do you need to sit down?"

"Oh, Steve, my ribs are killing me. It feels less painful when I stand up."

Stevie said to Daryl, in an *I'm-in-charge* voice, "Enough waitin' for an ambulance. I've got four-wheel drive. I'm drivin' my truck down here and I'm takin' Kaitlyn myself."

Kate looked at Stevie affectionately, and mouthed the words, "Thank you."

"I think that's a better plan," Daryl agreed.

Stevie brushed a loose strand out of Kate's face. "Stay here. I'll be back in a minute." He walked away, then called back to the group, "Cancel the ambulance."

Daryl had already extracted his cell and was doing just that.

Kate said, "Let's keep walking. I need to go to my cabin so I can get a drink of water."

"I can fix that," Jake said, sprinting back to the beach blanket. He returned with a bottle of water. He removed the cap and handed it to Kate.

She took several swigs, then handed it back. "Can you hold this for me?"

Jake nodded.

Katherine hovered nearby. "What happened?"

"I got mugged last night."

"Mugged," Katherine gasped.

"I need to talk to the sheriff. I think the guy who beat me up was Arlo."

Katherine and Colleen exchanged curious looks. "Arlo? The owner?"

Kate observed the look. "What's going on?"

Colleen explained, "We think Arlo was murdered last night."

"What, you *think* he was murdered?" Kate asked, shocked. "Was he murdered or not?"

Katherine shrugged her shoulders and didn't answer.

"Hey, I didn't kill the guy. After what he did to me last night, I'd like to murder him." Kate reached for the water bottle and took another drink.

Jake asked, "Can you make a positive identification?"

"Well," Kate hesitated. "I couldn't see his face because he had a ski mask on, but I recognized his scent."

"Scent?" Colleen asked.

"He smelled like Old Spice."

"Old Spice? Is that a man's cologne?" Katherine asked.

"I'd recognize it anywhere. My dad uses it," Daryl added.

"Mine, too," Kate said. "First time I met Arlo, I smelled it and thought of my dad and my grandfather, who have been dead for a number of years."

"Where have you been?" Colleen jumped in.

"I got knocked out and woke up in this creepy trailer up the road from here. I found the beach and just kept walking until you found me," Kate struggled to speak.

Jake said, "It's okay, Kate. Take your time. You don't have to elaborate. Just get better."

"Thanks. Are you Katz's husband?"

"Yes, her one and only."

"It's nice to meet you."

Stevie drove up and jumped out of his truck. Daryl opened the passenger door.

Stevie gently took Kate's arm, Jake the other one. They walked her to the truck.

Stevie advised Kate, "It's gonna hurt like hell getting in, but grab the bar. When you say when, I'll push you in."

Once seated inside, Kate said, "Steve, I need your phone to call the sheriff—"

Stevie cut her off. "What you have to tell him can wait until I get you to the hospital."

Stevie shut the door and walked over to the driver's side. He climbed in behind the wheel.

Katherine, Colleen, Jake and Daryl had worried looks on their faces. They waved as the truck pulled away.

*　　*　　*

After Stevie and Kate left, the group headed for the beach blanket and sat down.

"We need to talk," Katherine said to Jake and Daryl.

Daryl spoke first, "Start from the very beginning."

"Oh, I can do that," Colleen said and began talking about Mum's wrong directions to the cabin.

Daryl gently touched her arm, "Sweetie, I mean, when you found the body."

"Oh," Colleen giggled. "Oops."

Katherine piped in. "Scout found it."

Jake asked, "How'd she get out of our cabin?"

"She tore a hole in the screen," Katherine said, then changed to a different topic. She ended by saying the sheriff didn't take Colleen and her seriously. "He said the next time I call in a bogus crime, he was charging me."

Daryl said, "Colleen filled me in on that."

"There's something cagey about the sheriff," Katherine said.

"Why do you say that?" Daryl asked.

"Because he didn't stay in Cabin Six long enough to check it out to corroborate our story."

Colleen added, "It seemed like he was there for only a few minutes, then he knocked on our door."

Daryl said, "It doesn't sound like good police work."

"What are we going to do?" Colleen asked.

Katherine finished, "At midnight, we're going to take a walk on the beach. We're going to approach Cabin

Six from the dune-side and see if anyone is home. If no one is, we'll go in and take a look."

Daryl countered, "Katz, that's breaking and entering. In other words, it's illegal."

"I know it is. I'm not serious, but we have to do something."

"I've got an idea. You guys stay here. I'm going to walk to the manager's office and see if he'll tell me who's in Cabin Six," Daryl said.

"Why?" Jake asked.

"Because if we know who it is, we can knock on his door, and see if he'll talk to us. I want to ask him some questions."

"Oh, we already know," Katherine said. "The cabin isn't rented this weekend. Misty, the manager, told the sheriff that Arlo was there — in Cabin Six — for a little while because they'd gotten into an argument. He didn't stay the night; he went back home."

"I'm confused. I thought Arlo was the manager," Daryl said.

"He's the owner," Katherine explained.

Colleen added, "He used to manage the place, but he quit because of health problems."

"Well, then, there's no need to ask who is staying in Cabin Six. Do you think this Arlo guy was playing the practical joke and not a bunch of teenagers?" Daryl asked.

"If he was, he's a good actor. He convinced Colleen and me that he was dead."

"I mean, maybe he thought his wife would come in and find him like that, to scare her, then they'd make up."

Colleen laughed, "Daryl, you can't be serious."

"I've seen cases like this before. Husband gets drunk; wife gets mad. Husband leaves wife; wife finds him. Husband pretends he's sick or injured—"

"Or dead," Katherine broke in.

"The couple make up. End of story."

Jake offered his two cents, "Katz, you have to admit, it does make sense. That's why when you two left Arlo, he simply got up and went back home."

"Jury is still out on that one," Katherine said, then added, "Oh, I'm done talking about this. Let's have some fun. Anyone want dessert? There's some strawberry strudel left."

"Yes," Jake said eagerly. He extended his hand to Katherine. "My lady?"

"Yes, kind sir."

Daryl took Colleen's hand, and the two couples walked back to the cabin.

Chapter Fifteen

A few hours later, Stevie and Kate returned from the hospital. Katherine, Jake, Colleen and Daryl sat at a picnic table in the back yard of their cabin. Scout and Abra were both on long leashes attached to a stake in the ground. They were busy rolling around in the sand, and making chattering sounds.

Stevie parked behind Kate's cabin and got out of his truck to help her inside.

Kate waved at the group, but didn't say anything. Stevie walked her to her cabin but didn't go inside. Instead, he came over to the group at the picnic table.

"How is she?" Katherine asked.

Stevie answered, "No broken bones, but a large contusion on her right side."

"What's a contusion?" Colleen asked.

"A big-ass bruise," Stevie said. "The ER doc gave her a shot for the pain. On the way back here, we stopped at the drug store and picked up several other meds."

Katherine asked, "Is she going to be okay?"

Stevie smiled, "Yes. The doc said she'd live another day, but she's to take it easy this week. Katz, can you check on her later? Maybe take her something to eat or change the ice in her ice bag," Stevie fussed.

"Where are you going to be?" Daryl asked in a tone that was slightly sarcastic. Colleen nudged him in the ribs.

"I have to get back to Erie. Salina has been texting me like crazy. I was supposed to pick her up at Margie's and Cokey's an hour ago."

"They won't mind. Shelly and Salina are best buds," Jake said. "I'm sure the girls are having a ball."

"We'll check on Kate. Don't worry about it," Katherine assured.

Stevie started to leave, but Daryl stopped him. "Did Kate talk to the sheriff?"

"Yes, she did. She gave her statement at the hospital. Weirdest thing, though. When Kate mentioned she thought the guy who attacked her was Arlo, the sheriff got his feathers ruffled, and said she should think more about that allegation before she signed her statement."

"That's because Arlo and the sheriff are friends," Katherine said derisively.

"That explains it," Stevie said, running his hand through his blond hair. "Anyway, got to go. You folks have a nice weekend. Catch you later."

Stevie left, and was only a few feet away, when Josh Williams, driving a GMC Sierra, pulled up behind Katherine's SUV in Cabin Three's parking space.

Stevie stopped dead in his tracks. He recognized the vehicle that had stopped by at the pink mansion and the man driving it.

Josh got out and rushed over to Stevie. "What the hell are you doing here?" he asked angrily.

"I could ask you the same," said Stevie. "So, this is the cabins on Lake Michigan, the ones you told my brother Dave about?"

"What of it? I manage the place."

"Manage the place," Stevie said cynically. "That's a good one. We both know that's a lie."

"Who are you calling a liar?"

"Let me give you a word of advice. You have a big problem with your love life."

"What's that supposed to mean?"

"Number one, she's married. Number two, the old man she's married to is not ready to kick the bucket. The dude is good with his fists. He particularly likes to beat up women."

"You're full of it."

"Maybe I am, but the old man ain't no geezer. I'm sure when he finds out you've been messin' with his wife, he'll kick the crap out of you."

Josh lunged at Stevie, but Stevie stepped aside and missed the blow. Josh lost his balance and fell to the sand.

Scout and Abra began shrieking their Siamese distress call. Katherine and Colleen ran to the stake they were tied to and unhitched their leashes. Then they grabbed the cats and rushed them inside the cabin.

Simultaneously, Daryl and Jake ran over to break up the fight.

Josh got up and threw another punch.

Stevie moved aside and missed it. "I've got no quarrel with you," Stevie said. "Back off."

"Yes, back off," Daryl said in a voice of authority.

"Who the hell are you?" Josh asked.

"I'm a deputy in another county—"

"But not this county, which means you ain't got no jurisdiction."

Daryl grabbed Josh by the front of his jacket, and within a few seconds had him leaning against his pickup truck, wearing handcuffs. "Jake, watch him. I'm calling this in."

Stevie stepped over. "Don't," he said. "He's on parole and he'll go back to jail over this."

"It was assault," Daryl said.

"He didn't hit me," Stevie countered. "Do me a favor? Don't call the sheriff. Let Josh go. I won't press charges."

"Yeah, Mr. County Mounty," Josh said belligerently.

Daryl unlocked the handcuffs. "Have it your way."

Jake asked Josh, "What are you doing here, anyway?"

"I came to see about fixing the water heater."

Katherine came back outside. "It's fixed, thank you very much, but aren't you a bit late?"

Jake motioned Katherine to go back inside.

Katherine gave Josh a disapproving look and returned to the cabin.

Josh brushed the sand off his jeans and got in his truck. He peeled out, which caused a cloud of sand dust to descend on Jake, Daryl and Stevie.

Stevie called him a jerk, then stopped to answer his phone. Speaking into it, he said, "Yeah, it's okay. You can stay over. I'll pick you up tomorrow around noon. Okay, baby cake? All right, then. Have fun. Daddy loves ya. Bye."

Jake was surprised at how quickly Stevie could change from an angry man about to do battle to a sweet father talking to his child.

Stevie put his phone back in his pocket. "Change of plans. Salina is staying one more night. Tell Katz she doesn't need to check on Kate. I'm staying the night." He walked away, throwing a wave goodbye.

Daryl called after him. "I didn't know you studied martial arts."

"There's a lot of stuff you don't know about me," Stevie said, stepping inside Kate's cabin.

*   *   *

A little before midnight, Katherine, Jake, Colleen and Daryl left their cabin and walked down the path to the beach. Jake and Daryl lugged two retro aluminum lawn chairs each, while Katherine and Colleen carried the Siamese.

"Scout, stop squirming," Katherine scolded. "It's hard to hold on to you." Scout wore a blue collar that matched her deep blue eyes. Abra wore a red one.

"Waugh," the Siamese sassed.

"I appreciate the full moon," Colleen said.

"Raw," Abra answered. Colleen kissed the cat on top of her head.

"Yeah, I'm glad it's bright so we can see where we're going," Jake chuckled. "I wouldn't relish falling down this dune."

"Like Katz did," Colleen laughed.

"No comment," Katherine said.

Jake wouldn't let it go. "Katz, you fell twenty feet—"

"I slid on my behind. The sand cushioned the fall," Katherine answered, embarrassed.

Colleen said, excitedly, "I've got an idea. Maybe we should borrow Kate's firepit and make s'mores."

Jake teased, "We could have done that but your fiancé ate all the chocolate bars."

"You didn't," Colleen said, laughing.

"Guilty," Daryl confessed.

Katherine said, "I'm nixing the firepit idea. I don't want the cats to get near it and singe their fur."

On the beach, Jake and Daryl set the lawn chairs in the sand. Daryl patted one of the seats for Colleen to sit down.

The Siamese became very excited and wanted down. "Waugh!" "Raw!" they called in shrill voices.

"Hurry up, Jake. I can hardly hold her," Katherine said, holding a determined-to-get-down cat.

Jake screwed in the pet stake — with a fifteen-foot tie out cable — in the sand, then tested to make sure it was secure.

"Make sure they can't get in the water," Katherine advised, thinking she didn't want a replay of Scout jumping in and doing a little late-night fishing.

Jake answered, "Swimming in Lake Michigan isn't allowed until Memorial Day. The water's too cold."

"I know that, Professor," Katherine teased, "but Scout doesn't play by the rules."

"Rules? You mean, we can't go jump in the lake?" Colleen teased.

"Sure, go ahead, if you want to get hypothermia. In April, the average lake temperature is between 37 to 46 degrees," Jake commented.

"Cuz, are you planning on getting a job with the park service? You sure do know your facts," Daryl teased.

Colleen laughed. "Scout has a fur suit. I'm sure she wasn't too cold after she dove into the lake."

Once Jake had attached each of the cats' leashes to the staked cable, Scout lunged to the very end of her leash and pulled the cable taut. Abra planted her feet in the sand and began crying.

Katherine moved over to the Siamese. "Don't you like the beach?"

Abra reached up to be held.

Katherine picked her up. "Okay, you can sit with me." She unhooked Abra's leash and placed the Siamese on her lap. Abra curled up and snuggled against her.

Jake sat down on the lawn chair next to her. "Katz, I think we should buy a vacation, home-away-from-home, cabin or house in this area. I love the lake."

"Not a bad idea. Do you think our other cats would love it here as much as Scout and Abra do?"

Scout trotted back. "Na-waugh."

Daryl chuckled, "Did that cat just say no?"

Scout nudged Jake's knee with her face. Jake picked her up. "Not liken' the sand?"

Scout sat on Jake's lap and faced the lake. Small waves were lapping against the shore.

"It's getting breezy," Katherine noted.

Jake asked, "Is this the time you saw the ghost?"

"Spirit," Colleen corrected. "Yes, it was a little after midnight."

"Where did you see it?"

"Over there," Colleen pointed to the very edge of the water.

Daryl asked, "What did she look like? Could you see her face?"

"No, she was walking . . . I mean gliding . . . down the beach, away from us," Colleen answered.

"How did you know it was a woman?" Daryl persisted.

"She had long hair that was blowing in the breeze."

"Breezy, like right now?" Jake asked, looking around.

"Exactly," Katherine answered. "When I first saw her, she was a translucent shape, then she changed into the figure of a woman."

"What kind of clothes did she have on?" Jake asked.

"A long, black dress. Why do you ask?"

Jake, always the historian, said, "If she was wearing Victorian clothes, that would date the scene."

Both Katherine and Colleen shook their heads.

Colleen said, "I was really concentrating on her face—"

"But we didn't see her face. At least, I didn't. She was walking away from us."

"We didn't have time to investigate . . ."

"Boo," Daryl shouted.

Katherine startled. "You scared me half to death," then to Abra, "It's okay, my treasure. Daryl was just kidding."

Scout jumped off Jake's lap and growled.

Colleen said tartly to Daryl, "Very funny. I'm not amused. I know you don't believe in the paranormal, so cut it out, already."

Daryl shot his hands up. "I'm innocent until proven guilty," he chuckled.

"Kate said the spirit only appears when there's going to be a murder in Seagull," Colleen said.

Katherine added, "Two years ago was the last sighting. There was a murder on the beach, this beach."

"If that's the case, I hope we don't see her," Jake said.

Daryl got up from his chair. "Who's there?" he asked.

"Not again," Colleen scolded.

They turned in their chairs and looked at the path to the beach. Someone was walking toward them, shining a flashlight. The beam from the flashlight was shaking erratically.

"It's me," Stevie called. "What are you folks doing?"

Jake joked, "We're waiting for a ghost. What are you doing?"

"Kate's a sound asleep, so I thought I'd take a long walk on the beach to get my steps in," he said, shining the light on his pedometer watch.

"Good idea. Enjoy your walk," Katherine said.

"Thanks, Katz. Good evening." Stevie passed them and trudged on the sand.

Scout followed to the length of the cable. "Waugh," she cried after Stevie.

Stevie reached down and petted her. He whispered to the Siamese, "Take care of your mommy."

"What did you say?" Jake asked.

"Oh, I was telling Scout how pretty she is."

"Aw, that was sweet," Katherine said.

Stevie left and soon the couples lost sight of him.

Abra jumped off Katherine's lap and joined Scout. They stood in the sand, and began swaying back and forth, in a macabre dance.

"Mir-waugh," Scout screeched. Abra caterwauled a shrill, wailing sound. The Siamese continued their dance, arching their backs and hopping up and down like deranged Halloween cats.

Katherine was the first one off her chair. She darted over to them. "Come to me, my treasures. There's nothing to be afraid of."

"Look," Colleen screamed, pointing.

A glowing translucent shape glided down the beach in front of them. It moved over the sand and headed in the direction where Stevie had just walked. When the shape touched the sand, it materialized into the figure of a young woman. She turned to the group and gestured with her hand to follow her.

"Don't be afraid," Colleen said. "She's trying to tell us something."

Katherine said frantically, "Jake. Daryl. Stevie's in danger. Go warn him."

Jake asked Daryl, "Are you packin'?"

"Yes, let's hurry. Colleen, Katz, go back to the cabin and wait for us there," Daryl commanded.

Katherine started to protest.

"Do what he says, Katz," Jake pleaded.

Katherine nodded.

Jake and Daryl tried to run to find Stevie, but the loose sand prevented their attempt to build up speed.

The spirit disappeared.

Katherine said to Colleen, "Help me get the cats back to the cabin."

Colleen hesitated.

"Please, let's do what Daryl said. He has a cop's instinct. He wants us to be safe."

"Yes, of course," Colleen answered, taking hold of Abra. "I trust Daryl with my life, but couldn't he at least have left me his cell phone?"

"Cell phone? He might need it."

"I mean for the flashlight."

Katherine scoffed. "There's enough moonlight to make our way back."

"When I get Abra situated, I'm going to find Daryl and Jake."

"Okay. Deal. I'll come with you."

Chapter Sixteen

When Stevie left the two couples, he headed toward the water's edge. There, he found the packed sand easier to walk on.

He mulled over the events of the last few days. He thought about his first date with Kate and how much fun they had, then today's disappointment. He was looking forward to their second date, then for reasons out of his control, it didn't happen. *What a nightmare*, he thought, *seeing Kate on the beach, injured.*

Kate knew he had done time. She seemed okay with that. Hell, that's where he'd met her — in prison. She helped him find an attorney for his divorce.

He wished he wasn't so suspicious. It was just his nature to question everything around him, especially when it came to people. He wondered if it was purely by chance that he had a date with a woman living in a cabin maintained by Josh. Did she seek him out on Facebook to set him up to do something criminal? It raised a red flag. Could he trust her? He was having serious doubts. He wasn't sure there'd be another date.

Besides, he rationalized, it would get old driving back and forth from Erie to Seagull to have a relationship. Why didn't he just hook up with someone in Erie? He sighed and said aloud, "Because of Katz."

Then, there was the stupid argument with Jake over Katherine. He wondered if he'd told her. He hoped not, because he didn't want anything to come between him and the woman he loved. It was so unlike him to show his emotions, especially to Jake. And, that silly thing he said to the cat. *I'm losing my mind*, he said out loud. *Take care of your mommy*, he repeated. Ridiculous.

He continued walking, and watched the waves lap close to his feet. Up ahead he could see a man, on the loose sandy area of the beach, dragging a body toward the water's edge. The man must have heard him, because he stopped.

Stevie increased his step, and was soon face-to-face with a man in his seventies, who was lifting a large rock. "Hey, what are you doing?" Then he looked down at the sand. There, Josh Williams lay dead with multiple head injuries.

Stevie lunged to stop the man from striking another blow. "Stop it!" he shouted. "He's down. He's dead. Take a step back."

The man turned and threw the rock at Stevie, who dodged it. He then lunged at Stevie and tried to put him in a chokehold, but Stevie flipped the man over his shoulder.

The man fell on his back in the sand.

"Stay down," Stevie ordered.

The man grunted, then got back up. "This is none of your business."

"It's my business when I stumble upon a murder scene." Stevie tried to extract his cell phone from his pocket, but the man reared up and head-butted Stevie with such force, Stevie crumpled to the sand.

The man picked up the rock to strike Stevie.

Daryl raced up. He pointed his service revolver at the man. "Put it down," he commanded.

"Don't shoot," the man said, letting go of the rock. "My name is Arlo Komensky. I own the cabins. I was taking a walk on the beach and heard a scuffle. I found that man over there bashing Josh Williams's head in," he said, pointing at Stevie.

Stevie sat up, rubbing his forehead. Jake ran over and helped him get to his feet.

Stevie said, "He's lying. He attacked me."

Daryl continued pointing his gun at Arlo. "I need to frisk you."

Arlo said arrogantly, "Be my guest. You won't find anything."

Daryl patted Arlo down with one hand. "Now, sit down and put your arms straight out."

"Hey, I'm an old man. It will take time." Arlo struggled, sat down and straightened his arms.

"Not like Frankenstein," Daryl said, not kidding. "Straight out at your sides."

Arlo did so.

Daryl cuffed one hand, put it behind Arlo's back and then cuffed the second hand.

"Can you help me get up?" Arlo asked.

Daryl continued to point the gun at him. "No. I want you to sit there until I tell you otherwise."

Arlo gave a defiant look, then twisted his body to face the lake. "Hey, Mister Big Stuff with the gun. You're making a mistake. Sheriff Earle will be here any second and he'll vouch for me."

Daryl put his weapon away. "See that man over there with the bruised forehead? He has a firm alibi, and four witnesses that will state he didn't kill Josh Williams."

"Are you the law?" Arlo asked. "You act like it."

"I'm a deputy from another county," Daryl said slowly, "trying to take a few peaceful days off from work. Then you came along, with your bogus story, and messed things up."

A woman ran along the top of the dune. She was very close to the edge. "No-o-o," she screamed. She tripped and tumbled down the dune. Jake ran over and extended his hand to help her up.

She shrugged it off. "Get out of my way," she shouted.

She rushed to the prone man and fell to her knees. "Josh, you can't leave me," she sobbed. She had her back to Arlo and didn't turn around until she heard his voice.

Arlo said to his wife, "I pity you, Misty. I hope you rot in jail."

Missy looked at Arlo and screamed, "You're dead. I saw you dead." For a moment, she was paralyzed with fear, then she got up and tried to kick Arlo, but Daryl restrained her.

"Calm down, Miss," he said.

Arlo said to Daryl, "You better arrest her. She's too gutless to kill me herself, so she had Josh do it. He stabbed me in the neck with a needle, but whatever drug was in it didn't do the job. When I came to, I heard them planning what to do next."

"I think that's something you need to tell your attorney," Daryl said.

Jake asked, "So where did this attempted murder take place?"

Katherine and Colleen walked up, shining their flashlights on Arlo.

Katherine said, "In Cabin Six, right Mr. Komensky? When my friend and I found you, you looked very much dead, but when the sheriff checked your cabin, you were gone. Where did you go?"

Misty looked at Katherine with wide eyes. "So, you were the one in the cabin," she said, incriminating herself.

Arlo answered defiantly, "I don't answer to you."

Katherine beamed her light on Arlo's face. "It was very traumatic for my friend and me. I think you owe us an explanation."

"I waited for Josh and Misty to leave, then I crawled to my truck, got in the back—"

"That's seems rather lame, as if the sheriff wouldn't search your truck," Katherine huffed.

"I pulled a painter's tarp over me and slept it off. I didn't wake up until a few hours ago."

"Is that when you murdered Josh?" Stevie asked.

"It was self-defense."

"Self-defense," Stevie mocked. "You murdered an unarmed man. Tell that one to a jury."

"He was armed when he attacked me in my cabin. I got the better of him and tied him up. He got loose, and I chased him down to the beach."

"I think that's something else you need to discuss with your lawyer," Daryl said. "Now shut up, Arlo."

The sound of sirens blared down the lake access road to the beach. Vehicle headlights and flashing red lights lit up the scene. Sheriff Earle's Dodge Durango was first, followed by his deputy driving a second one. They climbed out of their vehicles and walked over to Arlo.

The sheriff asked his friend, "Are you packin'?"

"I left it back in the cabin."

"On the phone, you said Mr. Williams was restrained. Why is he now lying dead on the beach?" the sheriff asked angrily.

"He got loose," Arlo said innocently.

The sheriff noticed Arlo's ashen complexion. "Are you okay?"

"Is he okay?" Misty stormed. "He murdered Josh in cold blood."

"Ah, the unfaithful wife speaks. Misty, you're under arrest. Deputy Howard, cuff her and take her back to the department."

"You can't do that," Misty protested. "I haven't done anything."

"Oh, I can do that. For starters, I'm charging you with the attempted murder of your husband."

"You have nothing on me."

"Deputy, cuff her, then put her in the back of your vehicle. After you've done that, call the coroner. She needs to get over here pronto."

Arlo said, "Arrest that man over there. He pointed a gun at me." He indicated Daryl.

The sheriff asked Daryl, "Is this true?"

"My name is Deputy Daryl Cokenberger. I'm an off-duty deputy in Brook county. I pulled my weapon because Arlo Komensky was trying to bludgeon this gentleman over there, with a rock," he said, pointing at Stevie. "The rock is on the sand, right there," Daryl finished.

"Deputy Cokenberger, did you fire your weapon?"

"No, Sir."

"Okay, then, you know the drill. Slowly take your weapon out and hand it to me butt-first. After you've done that, I want to see some ID."

Daryl relinquished his revolver to the sheriff, then presented his badge and ID.

"I'll need your statement, too," he said, handing the gun back to Daryl.

"Yes, Sir," Daryl said.

"I take it the handcuffs on Arlo are yours?"

"Yes."

"I'll see to it that you get them back."

"Appreciate it."

The sheriff moved over to Jake. "Who are you?"

"I'm Daryl's cousin. We're staying in Cabin Three for a few days."

"Oh, with Ms. False Reporting," the sheriff said, looking at Katherine, "and the red-haired Irish gal."

Katherine said, "As it turns out, I wasn't false reporting."

"Yes, I got that part," the sheriff said, then addressed the group. "Alrighty, then. Listen up, folks. I'll need everyone's statements," he said in his booming voice. Then he said to Stevie, "Do you need an ambulance? That's a nasty bruise on your forehead."

"I'm good," Stevie said. "Sheriff, can I talk to you privately?"

"Hell, you're among friends. Spit it out."

Stevie looked over at Katherine, then looked down, ashamed. "Josh Williams was my cellmate in prison. A few weeks ago, he came to the place where I was working and wanted me to get him a drug."

"What drug was that?"

"Potassium chloride."

"Why did he think you'd have it?"

"I used to deal in drugs, but I don't anymore."

Katherine walked over to Stevie and the sheriff and said, "I didn't know Josh's name at the time, but it was my house that Stevie was working in. I saw Josh and Stevie talking about something. Stevie became very irate and told Josh to leave, then Josh ran over my bicycle—"

"Mother of pearl, the soap opera continues," the sheriff said sarcastically. "Can you all play nice and go down to the department and write down your statements? I've seen and heard just about enough."

The sheriff stepped over to Arlo and put his hand on his arm. "Stand up," he said. "Arlo Komensky, I'm arresting you on the suspicion of homicide. You have the right to remain silent—"

Arlo interrupted. "He was messin' with my wife. I had the right to kill him."

The sheriff said irritably, "Shut up and let me finish. You have the right to remain silent. Anything you say can and will be used against you in a court of law. You have the right to have an attorney. If you cannot afford one, one will be appointed for you by the court."

"I can explain everything," Arlo continued. "We've been friends for so many years. Doesn't that count for something?" Arlo pleaded.

"Give it a rest. Tell it to your lawyer. Right now, I'm not your friend. I'm the law, so quit while you're ahead."

The sheriff pushed Arlo in the back of his SUV and closed the door.

Katherine said to Stevie, "Jake and I are taking you to the ER."

"I'm good. I ain't dyin' so save me some bucks. I ain't got no insurance."

"Ain't got no," Katherine repeated. "I haven't heard you talk like that in months. You definitely need to see a doctor."

Jake said, "Come on, Stevie, we're taking you whether you like it or not."

"I suppose," Stevie said reluctantly.

The sheriff called from his vehicle. "After you do that, I want to see all of you in my office."

"Yes, Sir, we'll do that," Jake answered for the group. "But where is it?"

"Downtown Seagull, next to the McDonald's. Big old sign out front says Sheriff's Department."

Two more vehicles pulled up. One of them was the coroner, the second was another deputy.

Jake and Katherine each took one of Stevie's arms and escorted him up the lake access road. When they got to the top of the dune, Jake asked Katherine, "Do you have your keys on you? I'll go get the Outback and come back for the two of you."

Katherine fished the keys out of her pocket. Jake took them and left.

"Stevie, do you want to sit down?" she asked.

"Katz, I've got something on my chest. I need to tell you."

"What's that?"

"I was very rude to Jake earlier today. I said some things I regret saying."

"No worries. Jake said he felt bad, because he was the one who started it. Whatever you two argued about, I don't want to know. It's between the two of you."

"But," Stevie began, trying to find the right words, then he changed his mind. "Okay, we're good then."

"Oh, and Stevie, don't buy me any more gifts and put them on my front porch."

"What are you talking about?" he asked guiltily.

"The bike."

"What bike?"

"You didn't put a bike on my porch?"

"No, you told me not to."

"Well, who did?"

Stevie shrugged his shoulders. "I'll come clean. When I told Salina about it, she insisted we buy you a bike. So, there you have it. Take it like a secret Santa gift."

"That was so sweet," Katherine gushed. "But can you tell Jake about Salina giving me the bike?"

"Yep, will do."

Back on the beach, Daryl walked over to Colleen and put his arm around her. "Come on. Let's head back to the cabin," he said.

On the way, he stopped, took her in his arms and kissed her hard on the lips.

Colleen fell against him.

Daryl stroked her hair. "You were quiet back there," he said.

"I was too scared to talk. I didn't know if that Misty woman had a concealed gun or if Arlo would get free and hit you with a rock. And, that wasn't just a rock. That was the size of a boulder."

Daryl laughed. "I love it when you embellish things."

Colleen laughed nervously. "Daryl, I've made up my mind about the wedding."

"We don't need to talk about it now. You've been through a shock."

"I need to get it off my shoulders," Colleen countered.

"Okay, I'll let ya."

"I want to get married in the church I attended when I was growing up in Queens. I've already talked to the event scheduler, and he said there were slots open in July."

"Slots? What does that mean? Lottery?"

"Days, silly. Will that work for you?"

"Well, yes, that part works, but a lot of my family won't be able to attend. It costs a ton of money to fly to New York, stay in a hotel. We ain't rich," Daryl explained.

"I understand. Mum will probably want to host a small reception after the wedding."

"That's nice of your mom."

"I was thinking we could have a second reception in Indiana."

"Now we're talkin'," Daryl said. "Where? You know which place I like."

Colleen smiled, "And your mom and your aunt like it, too. I'm warming up to the idea. You sold me on the barn."

"Yee-haw," Daryl said, lifting her up and twirling her around.

"Put me down, you fool," Colleen giggled.

Daryl set her down and planted a kiss on her cheek. "We're going to have the best reception with country music, country dancin' and country food."

Colleen kidded, "To think I'm marrying a good ol' country boy."

"Well, this ol' country boy needs some sleep. Let me fire up the Impala. Let's go to the Sheriff's Department, and get this thing over with. I'm exhausted."

"Me, too," Colleen said, yawning.

Chapter Seventeen

Two Weeks Later

Jake vied to find a parking place at the Erie Diner.
The diner was busy with the breakfast crowd. "Well, looky
there," he said to Katherine, riding shotgun. "That's
Jimbo's truck. And, it looks like his cronies at the liars'
table are here, too." He parked. "Okay, we'll wait for
Stevie and Kate to show up, then we'll all walk in
together."

"Are you sure that won't give Jimbo a heart
attack?"

"Hope not. But, he and his lying buddies need to
see that my wife is not having an affair."

"True," Katherine said. "Oh, there they are."

Stevie drove up in his work vehicle. He waved, got
out and walked over to the passenger door. He helped Kate
get out of the van.

Jake climbed out of the Jeep. Katherine had already
gotten out and walked toward the couple.

"Hello, you two. I'm so glad you made it, Kate.
How are you feeling?"

"A little sore, but that's to be expected."

Jake said conspiratorially, "Katz and I will go in first. We'll walk right over to Jimbo. You two follow."

"Sounds like a plan," Stevie said, taking Kate's hand.

Jimbo sat with his back to the diner's front door and didn't see the group walk in. He was talking animatedly about something to the other men at the liars' table, when Buster, sitting across the table, looked up with a shocked expression.

Everyone in the diner stopped talking and focused their attention on the table in the center of the room.

"What's a-matter-with-you? It's a funny story I'm tellin'," Jimbo said.

"Look behind ya," Clarence advised.

Jimbo turned in his seat. "Oh, hello, Professor Jake and Mrs. Professor." His face reddened.

Jake and Katherine didn't answer, but stood waiting for Stevie and Kate to walk in.

Stevie directed Kate to the liars' table. "Howdy, Jimbo. I want you to meet my friend, Kate Allen."

"Oh, my," Jimbo said with his mouth agape. He did a double-take, looking from Kate to Katherine.

"Sorry we missed you at the Rensselaer barbecue joint," Stevie continued. "It was downright unfriendly of you to not come over and say howdy," Stevie said firmly.

"Oh, my, my," Jimbo said with a stammer. "Pleased to meet you, Kate. You look just like Professor Jake's wife. Are you two related?"

Kate shook her head. "No," she answered.

Stevie's face clouded. "I think you owe us an apology for the lie you spread about us."

"What lie was that?" Jimbo asked, playing dumb.

"Better honor up and apologize," Buster advised.

Ruby observed the situation and rushed over, menus in hand. "Hey Jake, why don't you bring your party over to a booth. Got one with your name on it."

Jake didn't answer. Katherine tugged his sleeve and led him to the booth. They sat down side-by-side.

Jimbo fumbled for the right words, "I meant no harm. I'm sorry."

Stevie said, "Say it louder. Tell everyone in the diner what you said about me and Katherine Cokenberger, and how it isn't true."

Jimbo said in a loud voice, "Folks, I need glasses. What I said about Jake's wife being with Stevie Sanders was said in error. I was mistaken."

"And?" Stevie asked. "Something else you want to say."

"It won't happen again."

"Apology accepted." Stevie directed Kate to the booth with Jake and Katz.

The diner buzzed with everyone talking at the same time about what had just happened.

Ruby bustled over to the booth and took their orders, then went to the kitchen.

After they finished eating, Katherine asked Kate, "What are your plans? Are you going to continue staying at the cabin?"

Kate nodded. "Yes, I am. I got a surprise call from Misty's attorney. Misty wants me to manage the place until she gets out—"

Jake interrupted, "Will that be any time soon?"

"Her attorney is confident he can get her off."

"How?" Katherine asked. "She conspired to murder her husband."

"Misty claims she told Josh about Arlo's bad heart, but, Josh came up with the idea of murdering him."

"Josh is not exactly around to give his side of the story," Jake said sarcastically. "What was his motive?"

"He wanted to marry Misty, but was afraid she'd lose her money and the cabins in a divorce," Kate explained.

Stevie offered, "Plain and simple. Arlo had to die," then he said to Katherine, "That day Josh ran over your bike, he asked me to get him potassium chloride, the injectable kind. I told him to take a hike. I guess he found a dealer who'd sell it to him."

Jake noted, "That's one of the drugs used in lethal injections."

"What does it do?" Katherine asked.

"It stops the heart," Kate shuddered.

Katherine asked, "Will Arlo testify against Misty? After all, he heard Josh and Misty discussing his murder when he was almost comatose from the injection."

"Arlo recanted his statement to the sheriff. He said that Misty was very upset by his near-death. He didn't think she wanted to kill him, but wanted to run away with

Josh. When that didn't pan out, she became desperate," Kate said, shaking her head. "It's a mess."

"How did you find this out?" Jake asked.

"I have a friend who works for the newspaper. He read the statement."

"If Misty didn't conspire with Josh to kill Arlo, how will investigators corroborate what she's saying?" Katherine asked.

"Cell phone records match the date and time Misty said she told Josh to not go through with the murder," Kate began. "The night I tried to return Arlo's wallet, Misty was acting very strange. She had a black eye. She was hostile to me, which she has never been before. I went back to my cabin and was attacked."

"By Arlo," Jake said.

"My mistake. It wasn't Arlo. Misty told her attorney that Josh attacked me."

"Josh?" Katherine asked, surprised.

"It goes to show. I shouldn't have been so quick to accuse Arlo when I didn't even see his face."

"Because of the ski mask," Jake added. "What about the Old Spice scent?"

"Oh, geez, I was hoping that everyone would forget I said that. I'm so embarrassed that I accused a man because of his scent."

"But, you did smell it?"

"Yes, I did, but smelling it, and then accusing someone of assault because of their cologne, are two different things."

"Did Misty tell her attorney why Josh assaulted you?" Katherine asked.

"She said that Josh overheard the conversation between Misty and me at the office. He followed me to get the wallet because he didn't want me returning it to Arlo when he was going to murder him."

Katherine interjected, "But Josh assaulted you outside your cabin. You said you were looking for your keys when he attacked you, which means you were trying to get inside your cabin—"

"And not go to Cabin Six to return the wallet," Jake finished.

Stevie said, "Josh wasn't very smart. He was a habitual criminal and kept getting busted for the same type of crime."

"Arlo stated that when Josh jabbed him in the neck with the needle, he passed out immediately. He said when he came to, Misty and Josh were standing over him. Misty was crying, but Josh showed no remorse."

"I guess that shows that Misty did care about her husband," Katherine said.

Jake said, "We'll just have to wait and see how things turn out."

"Which brings me to my news," Kate said. "I've taken an accountant job in Michigan City. I start in September."

"Congratulations," Jake said.

"That's great news," Katherine said, not really meaning it. She looked at Stevie for his reaction.

He looked back with sad eyes. He motioned for Ruby to come over. "We need our checks, please."

Ruby tore off two orders from her pad. "You folks come back now, ya hear?"

"Thanks, Ruby," Stevie said, then to Kate, "We better get going. "I don't want to hit the rush hour traffic in Merrillville driving you back."

Kate grabbed her purse and said, "Katz, thanks for everything. Jake, you too."

"You're welcome," Katherine said.

"Listen, when Arlo's and Misty's cases go to trial, I'm sure you'll be called to testify, especially you, Katz. If you need a place to stay, you're welcome to stay in one of the cabins."

Jake and Katherine answered simultaneously, "No."

Kate was taken aback. "Why?"

Katherine said, "Thank you for your kind offer, but I never want to see the Seagull ghost again. Twice was enough."

"Understood," Kate said.

Stevie headed to the cashier and paid. Kate followed him. They left without looking back at the booth.

Katherine reached for Jake's hand and intertwined her fingers with his. "It doesn't look like Kate and Stevie will hook up."

"You never can predict matters of the heart," Jake said, then added, "I don't think they will, either."

Ruby brought over a large wedge of coconut cream pie and set it down on the table. "It's on the house," she smiled, refreshing their coffee cups. "*Bon appetit*," she said, moving to the next table.

Jake called after her, "Thanks."

Katherine dove into hers. She closed her eyes and blissfully looked up at the ceiling. "The best ever."

"Better than the first time you had it here?"

Katherine beamed at Jake with deep affection. "No, not as good. I'll never forget that day. It was pouring down rain and we were at the library. You came to my rescue and offered to drive me home. Somehow we ended up at the diner instead."

"It was love at first sight," Jake said.

"Was it really?" she asked.

"Yes," he said, taking a bite. "This may be the second-best piece of pie ever."

Ruby returned carrying a small bag. "This is a little treat for the cats."

"That's so thoughtful," Katherine cooed.

"It's ham bits. My cat loves it," she said, moving away.

"Speaking of cats," Jake said, "I'm going to check out our new home security app."

"Fun. Let's see how our cats play when the mice are away."

Jake put down his fork and picked up his cell phone. He punched in the security code and scrolled through several screens. Cameras were stationed in various places at the pink mansion, but he was looking for the one in Katherine's office.

"Bull's eye," he said. "But no cats in your office."

"There're probably on the sun porch."

Jake scrolled to a different camera location. "Nope, not there."

"I bet I know where they are?"

"Where?"

"Check your office in the attic. Scout, Houdini-cat extraordinaire, probably unlocked the door — again — and opened it for her co-conspirators to get up there."

Jake pulled up the screen, and chuckled.

"What's so funny?"

"You're right. Lilac and Abby are on the perch over the turret windows. Iris, Dewey and Crowie are on the windowsill."

"Where's Scout and Abra?"

Jake lowered his voice. He didn't want the other diners to hear him. He put his phone down on the table and rotated it to Katherine. "Scout has her paw on the mouse."

"She's surfing the web," Katherine whispered.

"Take a screenshot."

Jake picked up his phone, took the pic, then moved his fingers to enlarge it.

"What are you doing?"

"I want to see what's on the monitor."

"Can you tell in the picture?"

Jake laughed loudly.

Everyone in the diner turned in their seats and looked their way.

"Shhh," Katherine whispered. "Everyone is staring at us."

"Ruby," Jake called. "Bring us a take-out box. We need to leave."

"Right-o," Ruby said, standing at the next booth.

Katherine said, "Show me the picture."

Jake grinned ear-to-ear, and handed his phone to Katherine.

Katherine studied the screen on the monitor. "Oh, my goodness. It's a fish."

"I think Scout is sending us a message."

"That she wants to fish in the lake again?"

Jake shook his head. "I don't think Scout and Abra liked the lake, especially the ghost."

"Then the message could only mean one thing."

"What's that?"

"It's time to go home and feed them," she giggled.

Jake laughed and put his arm around Katherine. "I love you, Sweet Pea," he proclaimed in a loud stage actor's voice, so the patrons at the diner would hear him.

"I love you, too!" Katherine answered.

Jake wrapped his arms around her and gave her a big kiss.

Ruby came to their booth and cleared her throat. "Am I interrupting anything?" She laughed, then handed them the take-out box.

Jake said, "I'll settle up later. Right now, Katz and I need to make our grand exit."

Ruby chuckled and walked over to the liars' table. "Just thought you boys would want to know. Professor Jake and Katz are leaving."

Jake got out of the booth; Katherine did the same.

Jake swept her off her feet, and carried her out of the restaurant. She buried her face in his neck.

Inside, people clapped and cheered.

Outside, Katherine said, "You can put me down."

"Yes, my lady, but first, how about another kiss?"

Dear Reader . . .

Well, did you enjoy it? I hope so. I had fun writing it.

Thank you so much for reading my book.

I love it when my readers write to me. I try to answer all emails within twenty-four hours.

Email me at: karenannegolden@gmail.com

For all of you, who have written reviews on Amazon and/or Goodreads, thank you so much. I very much appreciate it.

I love to post pictures of my cats on my Facebook pages, and would enjoy learning about your pets as well. Follow me @ https://www.facebook.com/karenannegolden

If you are new to the series, the following pages describe my other books. If you love mysteries with cats, don't miss these action-packed page turners.

Thanks again.

Karen

The Cats that Surfed the Web

Book One in *The Cats that . . .* Cozy Mystery series

If you haven't read the first book, *The Cats that Surfed the Web*, you can download the Kindle or paperback version on Amazon.

With over five-hundred Amazon positive reviews, "The Cats that Surfed the Web," is an action-packed, exhilarating read. When Katherine "Katz" Kendall, a career woman with cats, discovers she's the sole heir of a huge inheritance, she can't believe her good luck. She's okay with the conditions in the will: Move from New York City to the small town of Erie, Indiana, live in her great aunt's pink Victorian mansion, and take care of an Abyssinian cat. With her three Siamese cats and best friend Colleen riding shotgun, Katz leaves Manhattan to find a former housekeeper dead in the basement. There are people in the town who are furious that they didn't get the money. But who would be greedy enough to get rid of the rightful heir to take the money and run?

Four adventurous felines help Katz solve the crimes by mysteriously "searching" the Internet for clues. If you love cats, especially cozy cat mysteries, you'll enjoy this series.

The Cats that Chased the Storm

Book Two in *The Cats that . . .* Cozy Mystery series

It's early May in Erie, Indiana, and the weather has turned most foul. We find Katherine "Katz" Kendall, heiress to the Colfax fortune, living in a pink mansion, caring for her three Siamese and Abby the Abyssinian. Severe thunderstorms frighten the cats, but Scout is better than any weather app. A different storm is brewing, however, with a discovery that connects great-uncle William Colfax to the notorious gangster John Dillinger. Why is the Erie Historical Society so eager to get William's personal papers? Is the new man in Katherine's life a fortune hunter? Will Abra mysteriously reappear, and is Abby a magnet for danger?

A fast-paced whodunit, the second book in "The Cats that" series involves four extraordinary felines that help Katz unravel the mysteries in her life.

The Cats that Told a Fortune

Book Three in *The Cats that . . .* Cozy Mystery series

In the land of corn mazes and covered bridge festivals, a serial killer is on the loose. Autumn in Erie, Indiana means cool days of intrigue and subterfuge. Katherine "Katz" Kendall settles into her late great aunt's Victorian mansion with her five cats. A Halloween party at the mansion turns out to be more than Katz planned for. Meanwhile, she's teaching her first computer training class, and a serial killer is murdering young women. Along the way, Katz and her cats uncover important clues to the identity of the killer, and find out about Erie's local crime family . . . the hard way.

The Cats that Played the Market

Book Four in *The Cats that . . .* Cozy Mystery series

A blizzard blows into Indiana, bringing gifts, gala events, and a ghastly murder to heiress Katherine "Katz" Kendall. It's Katherine's birthday, and she gets more than she bargains for when someone evil from her past comes back to haunt her. After all hell breaks loose at the Erie Museum's opening, Katherine and her five cats unwittingly stumble upon clues that help solve a mystery. But has Scout lost her special abilities? Or will Katz find that another one of her amazing felines is a super-sleuth?

With the cats providing clues, it's up to Katherine and her friends to piece together the murderous puzzle . . . before the town goes bust!

The Cats that Watched the Woods

Book Five in *The Cats that . . .* Cozy Mystery series

What have the extraordinary cats of millionaire Katherine "Katz" Kendall surfed up now? "Idyllic vacation cabin by a pond stocked with catfish." It's July in Erie, Indiana, and steamy weather fuels the tension between Katz and her fiancé, Jake. Katz rents the cabin for a private getaway, though Siamese cats, Scout and Abra, demand to go along. How does a peaceful, serene setting go south in such a hurry? Is the terrifying man in the woods real, or is he the legendary ghost of Peace Lake? It's up to Katz and her cats to piece together the mysterious puzzle. The fifth book in the popular "The Cats that . . . Cozy Mystery" series is a suspenseful, thrilling ride that will keep you on the edge of your seat.

The Cats that Stalked a Ghost

Book Six in *The Cats that . . .* Cozy Mystery series

While Katherine and Jake are tying the knot at her pink mansion, a teen ghost has other plans, which shake their Erie, Indiana town to its core. How does a beautiful September wedding end in mistaken identity . . . and murder? What does an abandoned insane asylum have to do with a spirit that is haunting Katz? Colleen, a paranormal investigator at night and student by day, shows Katz how to communicate with ghosts. An arsonist is torching historic properties. Will the mansion be his next target? Ex-con Stevie Sanders and the Siamese play their own stalking games, but for different reasons. It's up to Katz and her extraordinary felines to solve two mysteries: one hot, one cold. Seal-point Scout wants a new adventure fix, and litter-mate Abra fetches a major clue that puts an arsonist behind bars.

The Cats that Stole a Million

Book Seven in *The Cats that . . .* Cozy Mystery series

Millionaire Katherine, aka Katz, husband Jake and their seven cats return to the pink mansion after the explosion wreaked havoc several months earlier. Now the house has been restored, will it continue to be a murder magnet? Erie, Indiana is crime-free for the first time since heiress Katherine, aka Katz, and her cats moved into town. Everyone is at peace until domestic harmony is disrupted by an uninvited visitor from Brooklyn. Why is Katz's friend being tracked by a NYC mob? Meanwhile, ex-con Stevie Sanders wants to go clean, but ties to dear old Dad (Erie's notorious crime boss) keep pulling him back. Murder, lies, and a million-dollar theft have Katz and her seven extraordinary cats working on borrowed time to unravel a mystery.

The Cats that Broke the Spell

Book Eight in *The Cats that . . .* Cozy Mystery series

When a beautiful professor is accused of being a witch, she retreats to her cabin in the woods. Soon a man dressed like a scarecrow begins to stalk her, and vandals leave pentagrams at her front gate. The town of Erie, Indiana has never known a witch hunt, but after the first accusation, the news spreads like wildfire. "She stole another woman's husband, then murdered him," people raged in the local diner. "She uses her black cats to cast spells to do her evil deeds!" But what do the accusers really want? How is Erie's crime boss involved? In the meantime, while the pink mansion's attic is being remodeled, Katz, Jake and their seven felines move out to a rural farmhouse, which is next door to the "witch." They find themselves drawn into a deadly conflict on several fronts. It's up to Katz and her seven extraordinary cats to unravel the tangle of lies before mass hysteria wrecks the town. Murder, mayhem, and a cold case make this book a thrilling, action-packed read that will keep you guessing until the very end.

The Cats that Stopped the Magic

Book Nine in *The Cats that . . .* Cozy Mystery series

This classic whodunit boasts a new cast of characters: a self-centered magician, a compulsive gambler, a sweet cat wrangler and her grandmother, a caring nurse, and a wealthy couple. How are their lives intertwined with a show cat named Abra? In 2009, two Siamese cats performed in Magic Harry's Hocus-Pocus show, in front of hundreds of devoted fans. But their lives were far from magical, and their careers were cut short when Abra was stolen backstage after a performance. Why did the magician increase the insurance on Abra days before she disappeared? Was Abra stolen and sold on the black market? Or did anonymous cat-lovers rescue her from a life-threatening situation? A wealthy tycoon wants a Siamese cat with a specific look for his dying wife. Why? Four years later, Abra ends up in an animal shelter. Where had she been during this time? Back in Erie, Indiana, Katherine and Jake work on borrowed time to piece the puzzle together before Magic Harry tries to take Abra away from them.

Acknowledgements

I wish to thank my husband, Jeff Dible, who edited the first draft of this book.

Thank you, Vicki for being my editor. You are the best.

Thank you so much, Rob. Your spin on the book cover really set the mood.

Thank you, Bob for your advice on ballistics.

Thanks, Ramona and Louie for beta reading my book.

Thanks to my loyal readers, my family, and friends.

The Cats that . . . Cozy Mystery series would never be without the input from my furry friends. My husband and I have many cats, ranging in ages from five to fourteen-years-old.

Dedication

To my nieces, Melissa and Megan. To my nephew, Kevin.

To my great-nephews Ryan, Aidan, and Ben.

And to my furry friends:

Redmond, Morgan, Buddy, Rusty,

Jesse James, Sasha, Ruby, Snookems,

Bruce, Baby Doll and Tommy.

Made in United States
North Haven, CT
14 January 2022

14798444R00143